COLLIE WITH A CARD

As Mandy crossed the yard she saw a flash of brown and white streaking across the field about a hundred yards away. "It's a dog," she said out loud. She recognized the famous shape and markings of a dog like Lassie. *A rough collie*, she told herself.

The dog was running swiftly in the direction of Lydia's farmhouse, its gorgeous long coat fanned by the breeze. It kept looking around, which made Mandy think it might be lost. There certainly wasn't anyone walking along with it.

She clapped her hands to get the collie's attention. "Here!" she called. "Come to me!" She clapped her hands again, but she shouldn't have bothered because the dog was already running toward her. "Good dog," she said encouragingly. And that's when she noticed that the elegant animal held something carefully in its mouth. Something white and flat and rectangular.

"Hey!" Mandy exclaimed. "You're carrying a letter!"

Give someone you love a home!
Read about the animals of Animal Ark™

COLLIE with a CARD

Ben M. Baglio

Illustrations by Ann Baum

Cover illustration by
Mary Ann Lasher

AN
APPLE
PAPERBACK

SCHOLASTIC INC.

New York Toronto London Auckland Sydney
Mexico City New Delhi Hong Kong Buenos Aires

Special thanks to Andrea Abbott

ISBN 0-439-68760-8

Text copyright © 2004 by Working Partners Limited.
Created by Working Partners Limited, London W6 0QT.
Illustrations copyright © 2004 by Ann Baum.

12 11 10 9 8 7 6 5 4 3 2 1   5 6 7 8 9 10/0

Printed in the U.S.A.   40
First Scholastic printing, January 2005

This book belongs: Ariel Taylor
to

Do not steal this!

ANIMAL
Where animals come first
ARK

//// Turn into lost and
found!

One

"Happy Valentine's Day to you, too, Houdini!" Mandy Hope laughed as the friendly black goat reached up to nibble her chin. It felt very ticklish, and although Houdini's teeth were big and sharp, Mandy was sure he wouldn't actually bite her.

The two had become friends after Mandy had saved the goat from being fatally poisoned. She'd found him lying next to a rhododendron branch and realized at once that Houdini had eaten some of the leaves of a plant that was deadly to goats! Luckily for Houdini, Mandy's parents were vets who ran Animal Ark, a veterinary clinic in the Yorkshire town of Welford. Mandy

1

had rushed to a nearby farm and phoned her mom. Dr. Emily Hope had come immediately to get Houdini, and together they had worked through the night to save him.

"I don't think he's kissing you, Mandy." Her best friend, James Hunter, laughed. James was standing just outside Houdini's pasture with his Labrador, Blackie. Behind them, the Yorkshire fields stretched as far as the eye could see, a carpet of green and brown speckled with the pale shapes of grazing sheep.

Unusually for Blackie, he was sitting quietly next to James, almost hugging his legs while he eyed the sturdy British Alpine goat on the other side of the chain-link fence. Houdini showed no interest in his canine visitor, preferring instead to keep nibbling Mandy's chin.

James patted the Labrador's head and with a mischievous twinkle in his eye said to Mandy, "I'm not sure that's a valentine kiss. Houdini's just making sure you're not worth eating!"

"Of course, you know all about Valentine's Day greetings, don't you?" Mandy teased in return.

James's ears turned bright red. "I told you before, I don't know who that card is from."

"That's what you say. But how can we believe you?" Mandy chuckled.

"What's all this about a card?" asked a dark-haired

young girl who was coming over from the farmhouse with a pail of water.

"Hi, Amy!" Mandy called back.

Amy was the niece of Lydia Fawcett, the proud owner of Houdini and eleven other goats at High Cross Farm. She was staying with Lydia while her parents were on a business trip.

"James got a valentine in the mail this morning," Mandy explained as Amy let herself into the next pasture and poured the water into a trough beside the gate. A billy goat named Monty, who was Houdini's son, trotted over and inspected the bucket as if he hoped it contained something more interesting than water.

"Show Amy the card, James," Mandy prompted.

"Er, I don't have it with me," James muttered. He bent down and fiddled with Blackie's collar as if it needed adjusting.

"Are you sure?" Mandy said, catching Amy's eye and winking at her. She stood on tiptoe to look over the fence and stared pointedly at James. "Then what's that sticking out of your jacket pocket?" As if he understood what Mandy was saying, Houdini peered through the fence at James and Blackie, too.

James's hand shot from Blackie's collar to his pocket. He tried to hide the telltale red envelope, but it was too late.

"Yeah, well, I do have the card with me." James turned so red that his neck matched the color of the envelope. "It's no big deal. I really don't care who sent it."

"So, let's see it," insisted Amy, trying to tug the bucket away from Monty who had the handle grasped firmly between his teeth.

James made a face and started to take the card out of his pocket, but he was saved by Blackie who began straining at his leash, trying to back away from the fence. Blackie wasn't usually afraid of other animals, but for some reason he was never too comfortable around goats.

"It's OK, boy." James tried to reassure his dog as Houdini nudged his bony forehead against the fence. "He can't get out. Ernie made the fence totally goatproof!"

Ernie Bell, a retired carpenter, had put the fence around the meadow to stop Houdini from escaping and getting into trouble on neighboring farms. As Lydia Fawcett often said, her prize goat wasn't called Houdini for nothing! Since the fence had gone up, Houdini had escaped only once, when a visitor left the gate open.

Mandy slipped her arm around Houdini's neck. "Cut it out, you big bully. Blackie's a friend, and it's about time you got used to him."

"Especially since it's Valentine's Day," joked Amy. "Everyone should be in a loving mood today."

Mandy couldn't resist the chance to have another dig. "Yep. Just ask James!"

"For goodness' sake!" James rolled his eyes. "February the fourteenth is just a stupid day like any other. It's only card companies and people selling flowers and chocolates who push the whole thing so they can make lots of money." He flicked aside some brown hair that had flopped onto his forehead. "It's just meaningless hype!" he declared in a grown-up voice. He reminded Mandy of what her dad had said earlier that morning when he'd remembered too late that it was Valentine's Day. "A lot of commercial nonsense," he'd muttered on his way out to buy Dr. Emily a box of chocolates.

Amy took an apple out of her pocket and gave it to Monty. "It's not meaningless," she protested, leaving the pasture and bolting the gate behind her. "I think it's romantic. I wish someone had sent me a card."

"If you want one so badly, you can have this one," said James. He reached for the anonymous card and quickly added, "But it's not like I'm giving you a valentine."

It was Amy's turn to roll her eyes. "You just don't get it, do you?" she said, and waved away the envelope that James was holding out to her.

"Hey, there, kids! What's keeping you?" Lydia's voice came from the wooden barn next to the farmhouse. She was standing at the barn door with her hands on her hips.

"We're coming," Mandy called. She shooed Houdini away from the gate and carefully let herself out. "We were just having a little fun with Romeo here." She grinned at James.

"Put a sock in it, Mandy!" James had obviously lost his sense of humor when it came to Valentine's Day jokes. He reached out to nudge Mandy, but she lifted her arm in time and fended off the playful blow.

"The truth hurts," she said, determined to get the last word in. And before James could say anything else, she ran off toward the barn.

James and Blackie charged after her, Blackie looking very relieved to be leaving Houdini behind. "I'll get you back, Mandy Hope," said James, panting.

When they reached the barn, Lydia stood aside to let them go through the huge, dilapidated double door. She was a slightly built woman of about fifty with short brown hair. Her hands were calloused from years of working outdoors, and she wore a faded green padded jacket and brown corduroy trousers that were held up with string.

Lydia paused to tighten the knot in the piece of string around her waist before going into the barn.

"Do you want me to find a belt for you?" Amy asked her aunt.

"No, thanks. This piece of string does the trick, and the goats don't mind what I look like," Lydia replied with a shrug.

A chorus of high-pitched bleating greeted them as they walked into the barn, and several heads popped out from the pens on either side of the central aisle. "Yes, we've come to feed you," said Lydia, her voice filled with affection. She loved her goats dearly, and even though she sometimes struggled to make ends meet, Mandy knew her precious animals were always in great shape.

Right now, things were looking up for Lydia. She'd recently been interviewed on the radio about the benefits of goat's milk. She had explained how healthy it is, and how people who are allergic to cow's milk can drink it instead. There are also other benefits, like the milk being low in fat and cholesterol. No sooner had the program been aired than Lydia started to get calls from people wanting to know where they could buy goat's milk. Health-food shops as far away as York had also contacted her to place orders.

Lydia could barely keep up with the demand, so Mandy and James came by as often as they could to help out. This morning, a Saturday, Mandy's dad had given them a ride to High Cross Farm so that they could take the goats some leftover vegetables they'd collected from the grocery store on their way home from school the day before.

"The nanny goats have all been milked," said Lydia, looking up and down the warm, airy barn. The floor of each pen was covered with fresh straw, and the stone aisle was swept clean, without a loose wisp of straw in sight. Two of the pens were empty, reserved for Houdini and Monty, but goats peered out from the others, their eyes bright with curiosity and their stubby tails wagging just like a dog's.

"We only need to give them their feed and fresh water, then we're done," Lydia continued. She went to the feed bins at the end of the barn. "It's getting cold, so I'll keep them all in for the night and let them out into the pastures tomorrow. I'll bring Houdini and Monty in later."

"Stay here, Blackie," James commanded, picking up a pail of water just inside the door.

"You're talking to empty air." Mandy laughed — Blackie hadn't even come into the barn.

James looked around, puzzled. "Where the —" He stopped as a black nose appeared at the door. Blackie was obviously taking no chances. He glanced inside just long enough to make sure James was still there, then quickly withdrew.

"Silly dog." James grinned, then started filling the drinking pails in front of each pen.

Armed with a shovel and plastic bucket, Amy inspected the pens for fresh droppings while Mandy and Lydia poured oats and barley into the food troughs next to the drinking pails.

"There," said Mandy when they'd fed the last goat, a friendly nanny named Jemima who had a long, thin stripe of white down her back. "Can we come help you milk them tomorrow?" she asked Lydia.

"That would be great," she answered. "I have a lot of orders to get ready. Not just for milk, but for soft cheese and hand lotion, too."

"We can help you with those, too," James promised.

"I don't know what I'd do without you." Lydia smiled, peeling off her black fingerless gloves and tossing them onto a wooden chest in the corner. "Now, what do you say to some hot chocolate and cookies?"

"Yes, please!" said James at the same time that Blackie, who was still waiting outside, gave a loud bark.

"Typical Labrador." Lydia laughed. "Mention food and they're all ears."

"I don't think that's what he's barking about," said James, going toward the door.

"No. It's more an excited there's-something-here-come-and-see-what-it-is kind of bark," said Mandy, who knew Blackie almost as well as James did. "I hope Houdini hasn't gotten loose again," she added in alarm.

They all ducked through the door into the chilly air and saw at once what Blackie was barking at. A stocky bowlegged man was coming slowly up the overgrown path that led to the farmhouse, pushing a bicycle. He wore a black quilted jacket and brown corduroy trousers that were tucked into his green boots. On his head was a flat tweed cap that he raised politely when he saw them.

"Afternoon, all," he called.

"Good afternoon, Mr. Cartwright," Lydia called in reply.

"Who's he?" asked Amy.

"An old friend of my father's," Lydia explained in a whisper. "They both went into goat farming at about the same time." She frowned. "I wonder what he wants? I haven't seen him since Dad died. He must be about eighty-five now, possibly even ninety."

Mandy, James, and Amy followed Lydia along the path. When they reached Mr. Cartwright, Mandy saw that he was out of breath, as if he'd cycled a long way. And he looked easily as old as Lydia had said he was. He had wispy gray hair, watery blue eyes, and his face was gaunt and lined.

He stopped, and, tucking his cap under his left arm, stretched his right hand toward Lydia. "It's been a long time, lass." He puffed while shaking her hand. He glanced from Mandy to James and then to Amy. "Are these your children?"

Lydia looked surprised. "No, these are my friends, Mandy and James, and my niece, Amy. I don't have children of my own. Don't you know I never got married?"

"You might have since I last saw you," said Mr. Cartwright.

"Well, I didn't," said Lydia, sounding both shy and gruff. "I'm not the marrying type."

"Nor me," said the old man.

"Do you still have goats?" Lydia asked.

"Yes," replied the old man, and Mandy thought she saw a shadow cross his face. "Two billy goats and seven nannies. That's why I'm here, actually." He looked across the yard. "Still in good shape, that barn your father built?"

"Good enough," said Lydia, sounding puzzled. "It keeps my goats warm and dry."

"Ah." Mr. Cartwright nodded, then fell silent while he scratched his balding head.

Mandy exchanged a confused glance with James. Mr. Cartwright still hadn't explained what he was doing at High Cross Farm after all these years!

Amy nudged Mandy with her elbow. "Maybe he has a secret crush on Aunt Lydia and he's come to ask her to be his valentine!" she whispered excitedly.

"Oh, please!" muttered James. "He's much too old for her."

"So?" responded Amy, looking hurt. "Aunt Lydia's lovely!"

Before James could say anything else, Mr. Cartwright cleared his throat and announced, "I'd like you to have my goats, Lydia."

Looking completely taken aback, Lydia echoed, "Have your goats?"

Mr. Cartwright nodded. "I'm too old to take care of them now."

"But I can't take your herd just like that, at the drop of a hat!"

"If it's about money, I'm not asking much for them," said the old man. "It's more important that they go to someone who will look after them the way I would."

Mandy expected Lydia to jump at the chance to increase her herd, especially now that there was such a demand for goat's milk. "What a great offer," she said quietly to James and Amy.

But Lydia didn't see it like that at all. "Thanks, but no thanks, Mr. Cartwright." She sounded apologetic but firm. "I don't have enough pens in the barn, or enough land fenced off for any more goats. And I definitely don't have the time to look after — what did you say it was — an extra half dozen?"

"Nine," Mr. Cartwright corrected her.

"Twenty-one goats in all!" Lydia shook her head. "I'd never manage."

"But you have lots of helpers." Mr. Cartwright nodded at Mandy, James, and Amy.

Lydia looked at him in disbelief. "They can't help me all the time. They go to school, you know!"

"I'd left school when I was this lad's age." Mr. Cartwright glared at James. "Earning my own keep, I was."

Mandy and James exchanged a brief look, but Mr. Cartwright noticed it and said firmly, "No time for loafing in those days. You kids don't know anything, I tell you." Turning to Lydia again, he said, "Are you sure? It's the best offer you'll ever get."

"It's very kind of you," Lydia said politely. "But if I can't take good care of the goats, I shouldn't take them on."

The old man seemed disappointed. He shook his head and mumbled something that Mandy thought sounded like *More's the pity.* Then he gripped the handlebars of his bicycle. "If that's your last word, I'll be going. Unless you change your mind, Miss Lydia."

"I won't." Lydia sounded adamant.

Mr. Cartwright swung his leg over the crossbar. But before he could pedal away, Lydia suddenly asked, "Would you like some tea before you go?" She bit her bottom lip as if she was embarrassed that such an old man had cycled all that way for nothing.

"No." He sounded proud, even though disappointment was still written all over his face. "I have to get back now. There are other goat farmers to contact."

"Then take the shortcut." Lydia pointed toward the gate on the other side of the yard. "There's a path across the field over there, behind Houdini's pasture."

"I'd forgotten that," said Mr. Cartwright, wheeling his bicycle around. "It cuts out a good couple of miles, doesn't it?"

Lydia nodded and took a bunch of keys out of her pocket. "There's a gate at the back of the field. I keep it padlocked, but I'll unlock it for you."

"James and I can do that," Mandy offered.

"Thanks." Lydia smiled and handed Mandy the keys. "Amy and I will fix our snacks."

As soon as Houdini saw Mandy and James approaching, with Mr. Cartwright wheeling his bicycle behind them, he trotted over to the fence.

"Houdini's pretty good at getting out," Mandy warned Mr. Cartwright as she slid back the bolt to the first gate.

"We'll have to go through the gates very carefully. You go in first, James. I'll go last and make sure the gate's shut."

James slipped into the pasture and, with the help of one of the dog treats he always carried, enticed Houdini away from the gate. While the goat munched on the snack, Mr. Cartwright pushed his bicycle over the grass to the other gate and Mandy made sure the first one was correctly bolted.

Still wary of the goat, Blackie gave James and Houdini a wide berth, preferring to stay close to Mandy as she followed Mr. Cartwright. They came to the far fence and Mandy unlocked the heavy padlock before swinging the gate open for the man. But even before the bicycle's front wheel was through, Mandy heard James shout, "Watch out!" In the blink of an eye, a hairy black-and-white shape shot past Mr. Cartwright and galloped onto the field.

"Houdini!" Mandy yelled, sprinting through the gate after him.

"You'll never catch him. He'll come back when he's ready," Mr. Cartwright called.

"No, he won't!" Mandy puffed, running even faster along the rocky track.

Blackie charged ahead of her, barking loudly as if he thought they were chasing the goat away! Seeing Hou-

dini hightail it across the field seemed to make him feel a lot braver.

But Blackie's excited barking must have sounded like a challenge to the goat because Houdini suddenly skidded to a halt, spun around, and hurtled back the way he'd come. His yellow eyes gleamed, and even Mandy felt a bit alarmed.

Blackie took one look at the goat and whirled around. He raced past Mandy to the pasture, where James was just coming through the gate.

"Whoa!" he cried as Blackie knocked him off his feet. He scrambled up fast, only to end up flat on his bottom again as Houdini rammed into him. "Watch out!" James cried indignantly, but Houdini was already halfway across the pasture.

"See? I told you he'd come back," said Mr. Cartwright when Mandy dashed past him. Chuckling to himself and shaking his head, the old man climbed onto his bike and set off down the path.

Meanwhile, Houdini was still in hot pursuit of Blackie. Mandy closed the back gate and snapped the padlock shut, then ran to help James rescue the Labrador. "Try some dog treats," she called.

"That's crazy," James puffed. "Blackie will never come for a treat now."

Mandy was trying to head off the goat by waving her arms in the air. "Not for Blackie. For Houdini."

"Oh, right." James took out a fistful of the dog treats and cut in front of the goat. "Here, you bad boy," he said, holding out his hand.

Houdini jammed on the brakes and, nose twitching, turned back meekly as if nothing had happened. Seconds later, he was crunching the treats out of James's hand.

Mandy patted her side and walked briskly toward the gate. "Come on, Blackie."

The Labrador didn't need a second invitation. He scooted over at top speed and squeezed through as soon as Mandy opened the gate. James dropped the rest of the treats on the ground. "See you later, Houdini," he said, and went to join Mandy and Blackie.

"You go into the house without me," Mandy told James. "I'll stay here for a while to make sure Houdini doesn't try anything funny now that he's had a taste of freedom." The fence was especially high, too high for the average goat to jump over, but Houdini had proved yet again that he was aptly named. He was a master of escape!

When James and Blackie had gone into the farmhouse, Mandy leaned her elbows on the fence and watched the goat for a few minutes. In the adjoining pasture, Monty pulled at his pile of greens as if nothing had happened. "Why can't you be content to stay in one place, like Monty?" Mandy asked Houdini.

The goat bleated as if to answer her, then flicked his tail and trotted over to his own heap of vegetables.

Mandy felt satisfied that Houdini had calmed down, so she started for the farmhouse, looking forward to a snack. Chasing a goat across the fields and pastures was hard work!

But as she crossed the yard she saw a flash of brown and white streaking across the field about a hundred yards away. "It's a dog," she said out loud. She recognized the famous shape and markings of a dog like Lassie. *A rough collie*, she told herself.

The dog was running swiftly in the direction of Lydia's farmhouse, its gorgeous long coat fanned by the breeze. It kept looking around, which made Mandy think it might be lost. There certainly wasn't anyone walking along with it.

She clapped her hands to get the collie's attention. "Here!" she called. "Come to me!" She clapped her hands again, but she shouldn't have bothered because the dog was already running toward her. "Good dog," she said encouragingly. And that's when she noticed that the elegant animal held something carefully in its mouth. Something white and flat and rectangular.

"Hey!" Mandy exclaimed. "You're carrying a letter!"

Two

"I wonder who it's for?" Mandy patted the collie's head and took hold of a corner of the envelope with her other hand. "Give," she said.

The collie either didn't know the release command or didn't want Mandy to have the envelope. He kept his mouth shut and moved his head to one side. But he wagged his bushy tail, which told Mandy that he didn't feel threatened by her attempt to take the letter.

"OK, have it your own way." Mandy smiled. She crouched down and felt around his neck. She hoped that under the dog's thick mane of hair would be a collar with an identity tag. But she found nothing. "Too bad," she murmured. "Now it'll be harder to trace your owner."

The dog seemed relaxed and not at all like a nervous stray. "You're in great condition," Mandy remarked, smoothing his long, silky coat, "so maybe you're not lost. Perhaps your owner sent you to deliver the letter, like a sort of maildog." She tried to see if there was a name or address on the envelope, but it was upside down in the collie's mouth and anything that might have been written on it was covered by the dog's lower jaw.

"Mandy! Aren't you coming in?"

She straightened up and looked around to see James and Blackie coming across the yard from the farmhouse.

"Who's that dog?" called James. Then Blackie spied the collie.

The dogs cautiously approached each other, looking away and slowly wagging their tails. Mandy had often seen dogs greeting for the first time, so she recognized the signals they were sending one another — canine language that showed they meant no harm.

"Who's this?" James repeated when he reached Mandy and the strange dog.

The Labrador and collie circled each other warily before touching noses. Blackie licked the new dog's mouth and seemed confused by the envelope.

"I don't know," Mandy admitted. "A special-delivery dog, it looks like." She pointed to the envelope.

"Is it a letter for Lydia?" asked James, frowning behind his glasses.

"I don't know. I can't see a name or address on it."

"It could just be an empty envelope that he found," James suggested. "Some dogs like carrying things around."

"Except that collies aren't really retrieving dogs," Mandy pointed out. "They're herders."

"I guess so." James nodded. "Let's take him in to Lydia. She'll probably know who he belongs to. He's got to be from around here."

Mandy agreed. "He doesn't look worn out from doing some kind of incredible journey! And for all we know, Lydia might even be expecting the letter."

But Lydia's expression when she saw the collie told Mandy right away that she'd never seen him before. "Where did *he* come from?" she asked.

"We thought you'd know," said James.

Lydia shook her head. "Never laid eyes on him." She was sitting at the big scrubbed table in the kitchen, sipping cocoa from a chipped mug.

Amy sat opposite her, eating a cookie that she put down as soon as she saw the dog. "He's gorgeous!" she exclaimed. "What's that in his mouth?" She jumped up to pet him, but the collie trotted straight to Lydia and deposited the envelope in her lap.

Lydia looked surprised. "For me?"

So she wasn't *expecting a letter by canine delivery,* thought Mandy.

"It's got to be for you," James said, pulling out one of the six unmatched chairs around the table. "Why else would he have turned up on your farm?" He moved the chair to face the dog, then sat down and leaned forward with his elbows on his knees. Blackie sat next to him, his tail thumping loudly on the stone floor.

"James is right," Mandy agreed. She sat beside Lydia on a red chair that wobbled on the uneven floor, and she bent down to pet the dog.

Lydia frowned. "None of this is making any sense at all." She picked up the envelope and turned it over, looking for a name. But it was blank. "If it was for me, it would have my name on the front," Lydia reasoned.

"Maybe whoever sent it forgot to address it," suggested Amy. She knelt down next to the dog and ran her fingers through the mane around his neck.

"Or didn't bother," Mandy added, "since the mailman — I mean mail*dog* — wouldn't be reading it."

"Why don't you just open it?" Amy prompted, looking up excitedly at her aunt.

Lydia turned the envelope over and over while absentmindedly petting the collie. He sat perfectly still next to her, his head resting in her lap. "It's wrong to open other people's mail," she said, voicing the solid values that were as much a part of her as her goats.

"But you don't know it's for someone else," argued Amy, her eyes shining. "And the Lassie dog *did* give it to you."

Lydia stared at the envelope. "Well, if it's not for me, then whoever it *is* for won't get it unless we find out who it's for," she said.

James scratched his head. "Sorry, can you go through that again?"

"Aunt Lydia will have to open the envelope to find out who it's for, otherwise that person will never get it," Amy explained impatiently.

"Oh, I see," said James, nodding.

Lydia got up and went over to an old pine dresser that stood against the wall. She opened a drawer and took out a letter opener, then sat down again and carefully slid the blade under the flap of the envelope.

Mandy held her breath, resting one hand on the collie's velvet-smooth head.

"It's a card," said Lydia, taking it out. The front was face down, so she turned it over. "For someone's birthday, perhaps."

But the picture on the front told Mandy exactly what

the card was, and who it was meant for. It showed a pair of black-and-white goats, nibbling a red rose.

"It's a valentine," Amy said breathlessly, echoing Mandy's own conclusion. "We should have guessed." Her face was flushed with excitement. "Someone wants to be your valentine, Aunt Lydia! Isn't that romantic?"

James rolled his eyes. "Girls!" he muttered.

Amy took no notice of him. "Look inside, Aunt Lydia," she urged, standing up to get a better view of the card.

Lydia seemed rather overwhelmed. She stared at the picture of the goats, her forehead creased into a frown. "How odd!" she remarked at last, slowly opening the card.

Mandy knew it was bad manners to lean over someone's shoulder and read their mail, but she was almost as impatient as Amy to find out who Lydia's admirer was.

Her impatience changed to frustration when she saw that the card was unsigned. "It's anonymous. Like James's," she said, disappointed. Inside the card, written in bold blue ink, there was only a big question mark underneath a short message.

"'The picture might jog your memory,'" Lydia read aloud. She raised her eyebrows. "Well, that doesn't make any sense at all!"

"It has to," Amy insisted, sitting down again and putting her elbows on the table. "Think hard, Aunt Lydia. What do two goats sharing a rose remind you of?"

"Nothing whatsoever," said Lydia. "And certainly no one in particular. So it can't possibly be for me." She bent down and patted the collie. "I think this fellow made a mistake."

"But he seemed to know what he was doing when he came here," Mandy argued. "Are you sure the card doesn't remind you of anyone? Someone from one of the agricultural shows, perhaps? Or another goat farmer?"

Amy clapped her hands together. "That's it! Another goat farmer. It's from Mr. Cartwright. I knew it!"

"That's ridiculous!" Lydia folded her arms and sat back in her chair. "For one thing, he's far too old for me."

James raised his eyebrows as if to say, *Didn't I tell you?*

Amy didn't notice. She was still trying to figure out who could have sent the card. "What about a boyfriend from long ago?"

"Nonsense," was Lydia's abrupt reply.

"Well, one thing's for sure," Mandy reasoned. "It's from someone who knows that you like goats. And he's got to be a nice person, because he's got such an adorable, well-behaved dog." She patted the collie, who twisted his head to lick her hand. "He could be one of your new customers — maybe even someone who heard you on the radio."

"Unlikely." Lydia stood up and went to put the letter opener away. "Anyway, this whole valentine business is a lot of nonsense. If a person likes someone, why send an anonymous card?"

"It's a good choice for someone who's shy around people," Mandy suggested. *Like you*, she was tempted to add to Lydia, but she kept the thought to herself.

"That's crazy," Lydia said. "I mean, what's the point in sending the card at all, if you don't put your name on it?" She bustled around the dresser for a moment, opening and closing drawers as if she couldn't concentrate on what she was doing. Then she came back to the table and picked up the card. "Waste of money," she muttered, sliding it back into the envelope before taking it to the living room.

Mandy wasn't convinced that Lydia really meant this — especially when she saw Lydia go over to the living room mantelpiece and carefully slide the card behind a pewter mug. Mandy was sure that, deep down, Lydia was as delighted as anyone to get a Valentine's Day card.

Anyone, that is, except James, who was nodding in agreement with what Lydia had said. "It's *is* a waste of money," he emphasized.

"Not everyone's a poor sport like you," said Amy, making a face at him. "I think it's great that Aunt Lydia has a boyfriend."

"I don't have a boyfriend," said Lydia, coming back into the kitchen. "That card's not for me," she snapped. The collie flinched at her sharp tone. "Sorry, boy," she said, patting him. Then she put her hands on her hips and frowned. "Now what are we going to do about you, Lassie dog? You can't stay here, you know. I have enough mouths to feed."

"He must know his way home," said James. "He'll go back when he's hungry."

This gave Mandy an idea. "We can follow him to find out where he comes from!" She twisted in her chair and looked at Lydia. "Then we'll find out who sent the card."

"I'm not so sure that I want to know," Lydia began. Then, remembering that she'd said the card couldn't be for her, she changed her mind. "But we *should* find out. Then we can give it back so that the collie can get it to the right person."

"That's sort of what I meant," Mandy said.

The collie stood up and sniffed around the floor. "Are you thirsty?" Lydia asked, going to the sink. She filled a plastic bowl and put it on the floor.

But the collie ignored it and went over to the door.

"It looks like he wants to go outside," said Amy.

No sooner had she spoken than the collie stretched up against the Dutch door, and in one smooth motion pushed the handle down with a front paw and dropped back onto all fours. As the top half of the door swung open, the dog leaped effortlessly over the closed half.

"Wow! That's good." James blinked in admiration as the dog disappeared over the top.

"Hey! Wait for us!" Mandy called, jumping up to follow the collie. But by the time she'd reached the door, the dog was already halfway down the path.

"Wait!" Mandy yelled again, running outside.

The collie paused and glanced over his shoulder at her before taking off again, moving as swiftly and smoothly as a shooting star. Unless Mandy and the others could fly, they'd never catch up with him.

"Rats!" Mandy stumbled to a halt and let her arms drop to her sides. "Now we'll never find out who sent that card!"

Three

"Has a rough collie been brought into Animal Ark lately?" Mandy asked her dad when he came to pick them up from High Cross Farm half an hour later.

Dr. Adam Hope steered the Land Rover carefully down the bumpy driveway. "I can't remember one," he said, dashing Mandy's hopes. "Why do you ask?"

She told him about the dog's appearance at the farm. "Of course, Lydia refuses to believe that someone could have sent her a valentine," she finished.

Dr. Adam turned onto the road at the end of the drive-way. "Why not?" He glanced at James in the rearview

31

mirror. "I mean, if James has a secret admirer, so can Lydia," he teased.

"Come on, Dr. Adam!" said James, slouching in his seat. "You know this valentine's stuff is a lot of garbage."

"I wouldn't say that," said Dr. Adam, surprising Mandy because it was *exactly* what he'd said that morning. "I mean, if you forget, you're in *big* trouble. But if you remember — even after you forgot — you're treated like a hero!" He looked at Mandy and gave her a lopsided grin.

"So the chocolates you rushed out to buy this morning were a big hit with Mom?" She chuckled.

"Yes, indeed," said Dr. Adam, nodding. "That's because she'd forgotten about Valentine's Day, too! And now I'm being taken out for a fancy dinner at The Forge tonight. Not bad, eh?"

"Not bad at all." Mandy smiled.

Dr. Adam braked, turned off the road, and stopped in front of a gate. A sign on it read UPPER WELFORD HALL. This was where Lydia's nearest neighbor, Sam Western, lived. He owned the most modern dairy farm in the district, and Dr. Adam was stopping by to give the cows their regular dose of worm medicine.

Mandy leaned out her window and pressed a button on the gatepost. The massive gate swung open, and Dr. Adam drove through and up the gravel driveway past landscaped gardens to the farm buildings behind the house.

"I wonder if Jane's here yet?" Mandy said as they climbed out of the Land Rover, leaving Blackie in the back with a rubber bone to keep him entertained.

Jane Jackson, one of Mandy's neighbors in Welford, had gone to York to study nursing. At first she'd studied human medicine, but recently, to Mandy's delight, she'd switched to veterinary nursing. Jane would be spending February at Upper Welford Hall as an intern.

"I think she arrived a couple of days ago," said Dr. Adam, taking the box containing the worm medicine out of the Land Rover. He gave it to James to carry, then led the way into one of the barns. "Simon called her this morning to arrange for her to come and look around our clinic." Simon was the nurse at Animal Ark, and Mandy knew he'd be a great person to tell Jane what his job involved.

The enormous ultramodern barn they entered reminded Mandy more of a hospital than a farm building. It smelled of disinfectant and was spotlessly clean, without even a blade of straw in the wide concrete aisle.

While Dr. Adam went to find Sam Western, Mandy stopped and stroked the neck of a curious cow who had stretched her head through the steel barricade at the side of the aisle. The glossy black-and-white animal seemed to enjoy the attention. She rubbed her huge head against Mandy's hand and then, quite unexpectedly, stretched forward and licked her right across her face.

"Thanks very much!" Mandy chuckled, wiping her cheek with the back of her hand. "But between you and the goats, I think I've had enough animal kisses for one day."

"What's this about goats and kissing?" said an amused voice behind her.

Mandy turned around and saw a tall, dark-haired young woman coming toward her. She wore a waterproof coat and green boots, and carried something that looked like a thin plastic rifle.

"Hi, Jane." Mandy smiled. "James and I have just been to High Cross Farm. You know, Lydia Fawcett's place."

"Yes, I know the farm," replied Jane. "I used to ride Prince up on the field around there."

Prince was a Welsh pony that Jane had been given for her tenth birthday, but she'd had to sell him when she went to nursing school. Mandy still got to see Prince from time to time because one of her school friends, Susan Collins, owned him now.

"Have you been to see Prince recently?" asked James.

"Yes. I popped in to see him yesterday, in fact," answered Jane. "He hasn't forgotten me! I had a lump in my throat when I saw how quickly he recognized me." She bit her bottom lip, but then she brightened up. "Anyway, he and Susan are great friends. She's taking him to a pony club meeting next week."

A door at the far end of the barn opened and Dennis Saville, Mr. Western's estate manager, came in. With him was a herdsman clad in light green overalls.

"Got the bolus gun?" Dennis called to Jane.

Jane nodded and held up the riflelike plastic tool. "I was just waiting for Albert." She smiled at the herdsman.

"Fine. I'll leave you to it," said Dennis, and he turned and strode back out of the barn.

"OK, Albert, let's get started," said Jane, taking the box of worm medicine from James. "I'll load the bolus gun while you put the first cow in the crush."

Mandy's jaw dropped. "Er, you are just giving them worm medicine, aren't you?" she said, a note of panic creeping into her voice.

Jane laughed. "It does sound sort of brutal, I know, but in fact, the whole procedure's completely painless. Look, this is what we call the crush." She took them over to a metal-framed structure at the end of the barn.

They watched Albert herd the first cow into the crush. Once she was in, he guided her head into a clamp that closed around her neck just behind her ears.

James winced. "That's like putting someone in the stocks!"

"Sort of," Jane agreed. "But I promise you it doesn't hurt the cow." Sure enough, the cow looked perfectly calm, blinking at her audience with her huge brown eyes. Jane reached into the box that contained the worm medicine and took out a bullet-shaped object about two inches long. She put it into the bolus gun before carefully pushing the slim plastic barrel into the cow's mouth.

"That looks like a useful tool," James remarked. Mandy guessed he was thinking of how Blackie usually managed to spit out his worm pills even when they were hidden in pieces of cheese or chunks of meat.

"Yes, it works very well," said Jane. "It shoots the pill right down into the cow's belly." She released the catch on the bolus gun, and the cow hardly flinched as Jane fired.

Albert took the clamp off the cow's head and opened the crush. The cow walked away calmly, as if nothing unusual had happened.

"That's incredible!" Mandy said. "She really didn't feel a thing."

Jane was preparing the dose for the next cow. "That's what I told you. It doesn't hurt them at all, and it means not one little bit of worm medicine gets wasted, since it all ends up in the cow's stomach."

Having watched the procedure and learned that it wasn't cruel or painful, Mandy and James pitched in by urging the cows into the crush one at a time, then back into the holding pen after they'd had their dose.

They were about to load the last cow when a terrible snarling stopped them in their tracks.

"What's that?" James demanded, looking toward the yard.

Mandy stared at him in dismay as she heard a barrage of loud, savage barks followed by deep growling. "Dogs!" she exclaimed. "And I think they're fighting."

Her first thought — her first *hope* — was that it was Mr. Western's two bulldogs squabbling over a bone or a toy. But when she ran to the door and looked outside, she had the shock of her life. Snarling like a pack of hounds, two much larger dogs were wrestling together, their paws locked around each other's necks.

"It's not the bulldogs!" Mandy cried. "It's Major and the collie from High Cross Farm!"

Without thinking, she ran to the pair. They were standing on their back legs, gripped in a tight embrace like a pair of prizefighters. Major, Sam Western's elderly German shepherd, had his jaw clenched and was shaking the collie's snout with all his might.

"Stop it!" Mandy yelled, feeling the blood drain from her face. She'd seen a few squabbles between dogs before, but nothing as serious as this. She couldn't believe that she'd let the collie run happily away from Lydia's cottage, only to see it end up here, being tormented by territorial old Major.

Oblivious to everything else, the German shepherd

and the collie jumped into each other again, their teeth flashing as they rammed heads.

"Stop it!" Mandy screamed again, feeling utterly powerless.

Mustering all his strength, the collie managed to back away without Major following. He sprang out of the shepherd's way and glared at him so that Mandy dared to hope that the fight was over. But a split second later, the collie threw himself at Major and bowled him over, snarling like an angry lion.

Major struggled wildly and heaved himself off the ground to snap at the collie's face.

The collie flung himself at Major again. With a loud thud, the shepherd crashed onto his side, yelping as his ribs and hip bones struck the hard ground.

"We've got to stop them before they kill each other," yelled James, and he lunged forward while Albert tried to wedge a yard broom between the dogs.

"Don't go near them! You'll get bitten," called Dr. Adam's voice. He ran out of the barn, and Mandy felt a huge surge of relief. Her dad would know what to do.

"Stop them, Dad!" she begged.

Dr. Adam looked around. "Get that hose," he ordered, pointing to an outside faucet.

Mandy raced over, grabbed the nozzle end, and dragged it over to her dad.

"Turn it on!" Dr. Adam said to James. "Full blast!"

James ran to the faucet and frantically twisted it on while Dr. Adam aimed the nozzle at the dogs. A jet of water shot out and hit the fighting pair with a deafening hiss. There was a surprised yelp as the dogs let go of each other and leaped out of the way. Dr. Adam kept shooting the steady stream of water until the dogs turned their backs on each other and gave up fighting. "OK, James," he said at last. "You can turn it off."

Everyone fell silent as they stared at the dogs. They were in a terrible state. Limping and whimpering, the collie collapsed in a pool of water, panting heavily. A few yards away from him, Major was sprawled on his side with his eyes closed and his chest heaving as if he could hardly breathe.

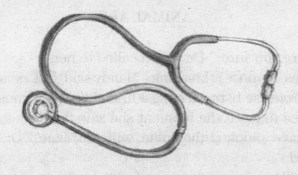

Four

Mandy ran forward. She knelt down in front the collie and petted the top of his head. "What was that all about?" she murmured, more to herself than to the dog. Her heart pounding, she stared at his trembling limbs.

The collie seemed to recognize her through his fatigue and limply wagged his tail. He licked his muzzle, and Mandy noticed with a jolt of alarm that blood was trickling out of his nose.

"He's hemorrhaging!" she gasped, looking around for her dad who was crouching next to Major. James was leaning over as well, peering at the exhausted German shepherd.

"Are you sure?" Dr. Adam called to her.

"Yes, his nose is bleeding," Mandy said, just as Jane ran out from the barn carrying a first aid kit. She must have rushed to get it the moment she saw the dogs fighting.

"Have a look at the collie, will you, Jane?" Dr. Adam asked.

"Will do," said Jane, and she knelt down next to Mandy. She did a double take. "Oh, no!" she exclaimed. "It's Ash."

Just then, Mandy was more concerned about the blood seeping from the dog's nose than his identity. "He's hemorrhaging," she repeated desperately, but Jane said calmly, "No, he's not. His nose has just been bumped. Look."

She took a wad of cotton out of the emergency kit and held it against the collie's nose. Then she took it away, and in the brief moment before the blood started to flow again, Mandy saw several nicks and bruises in one nostril.

"That'll need a few stitches," remarked Jane. "So will these," she added, casting her eye over some other injuries. "What got into you, Ash?" She sighed, dabbing the blood again.

"Ash?" James overheard Jane. "Do you know him?"

Jane took out a clean cotton ball. "Yes. He's Andrew's dog."

"Andrew Austin?" Mandy asked. Andrew was the manager of Sam Western's organic farm on the other side of the hill. Mandy and James had met him when they rescued a feral cat and her kittens, and Andrew had persuaded his mother to give them a home.

"That's right," said Jane. "I bumped into the two of them the other day."

"I didn't know he had a dog," said James, and he exchanged a puzzled glance with Mandy. She could guess exactly what he was thinking: Why would Andrew, a friendly, good-looking man in his late twenties, send Lydia Fawcett a valentine? But Mandy was too worried about the injured dogs to waste much time wondering about it.

"Actually, he's only had Ash for about two weeks," Jane continued. "He adopted him when the dog's original owners went to live abroad."

While Jane was talking, Dennis Saville came into the yard. "What's been going on here?" he demanded, his eyes bulging in his sharp-featured face as he stared at the two drenched and injured dogs.

Dr. Adam straightened up, looking grim. "There's been a dogfight, I'm afraid. We're going to have to get them both to the clinic right away."

Dennis's face creased with worry as he went over to Major. "You *are* in bad shape!" he said. He stroked the dog's head and then looked at Ash. He said to Jane, "I heard you say that the collie belongs to Andrew."

Jane nodded as Dennis stood up and started to jog back across the yard. "I'd better let Mr. Western know what's happened. He's in town, but I'll call him on his cell phone."

"Good. Let's get these two into the Land Rover," said Mandy's dad after Dennis left to make the call. "Get up," he urged Major, but the old dog seemed reluctant to stand. "Looks like we'll have to carry you," said Dr. Adam, and he signaled to James to give him a hand.

Ash was more willing to walk, even though he was limping badly, and Albert helped Jane and Mandy guide him to the Land Rover.

"We'd better keep them apart," Mandy said, and she opened the back door so that James and her dad could put Major in the roomy area behind the seats. Next, she helped Jane ease Ash onto the backseat next to Blackie. The Labrador sniffed at his new friend in surprise as if he realized the collie was not well and needed to be left alone. Blackie shuffled away and lay down at the far end of the seat.

James clambered in beside the German shepherd. "I'll ride here and keep an eye on him," he offered.

"Thanks, James," said Dr. Adam, carefully closing the door. "And Mandy, you can sit with . . ." He stopped when he saw that Mandy was already on the backseat, cradling the collie's head in her lap. "What made me think I needed to ask you?" Dr. Adam murmured with a small smile.

Jane climbed into the front next to Dr. Adam. "You'll need an extra pair of hands to patch these two up," she said, buckling her seat belt.

They arrived at Animal Ark just as Jean Knox, the receptionist, was closing up after morning hours. "Oh, my!" she exclaimed when she saw the dogs. She put down her handbag and frowned. "What a sorry-looking pair."

"Call Emily for me please, Jean," said Dr. Adam. "We'll have to work on both dogs right away."

"She's still in her examining room," Jean said, so Mandy hurried to tell her mom what had happened while Jean bustled over to the door that led to the residential unit. This was where animals who were too ill to go home stayed while they were being treated. "Simon, are you still in there?" Jean called.

"Yep. Just checking the patients before I leave," came the reply.

"You won't be leaving for a while," Jean told him. "There's an emergency."

"Be there in a sec," Simon called back.

Dr. Emily came into the reception area before Mandy

had a chance to look for her. "What's the matter?" she began. Then, seeing the two badly injured dogs, she flew into action. "I'll take care of the collie," she said to Dr. Adam, who nodded as he and James carried Major into the other examining room.

"Oh, and Mandy," said her mom, "phone Sam Western and the owner of this collie and find out when the dogs last ate. We'll probably have to anesthetize both of them."

"I'll do that," offered Jane, picking up the telephone directory on the reception desk.

Simon came in from the residential unit. "What happened?" he asked, wiping his hands on a paper towel.

"Bad dogfight," Jean told him, opening a drawer next to her desk to look for Major's file.

"I think Dad could use your help, Simon," said Mandy. "Jane and I will help Mom."

"Sure," said Simon.

Mandy and Dr. Emily took Ash into the examining room and lifted him onto the stainless steel examination table.

"Keep him still, please," said Dr. Emily, and Mandy gently held the collie's head.

Ash flinched as Dr. Emily examined a wound on his leg. "Sorry, boy," she murmured, cleaning it with disinfectant, "but that's going to need a lot of stitches." She checked a gash on his cheek and a cut to the soft fleshy part of his nose. "More stitches." She listened to his heart and breathing with her stethoscope. "Not too bad," she commented. Feeling Ash's tummy, she said to Mandy, "By the way, who does he belong to?"

Mandy told her.

Dr. Emily frowned. "If Ash is the wandering type and found his way to Sam Western's farm, Andrew will need to keep a closer eye on him in the future."

"I don't think Ash is a wanderer," Mandy began. She was about to tell her mom that the collie had been sent out to deliver a valentine card when Jane came in.

"I spoke to both the owners," she said, scrubbing her hands at the sink. "They're on their way."

"Good. Then they can give us permission to go ahead with the treatment. Ash definitely needs a general anesthetic," said Dr. Emily. "And by the look of Major, he does, too. I'd say he's pretty bruised as well. He might even have pulled a muscle, which is why he doesn't want to walk." She took the stethoscope from around her neck and put it on a shelf. "Oh, and did you find out when the dogs last ate, Jane?"

"At least six hours ago," answered Jane, drying her hands.

"That should be OK," said Dr. Emily. She patted the collie, who stared up at her, looking very sorry for himself. "I hope you'll think twice before wandering again."

Dr. Adam peered around the door. "How's your patient looking?" he asked. He was holding a file, and Mandy guessed it was Major's records. The German shepherd had been a regular patient at Animal Ark over the years.

"Not too good," Dr. Emily replied. "He'll need lots of stitching up, and some of those wounds will have to drain."

Dr. Adam looked at Ash and frowned. "Mmm. I guess he finished in second place," he said. "Major's got one or two bad scratches, and a cut above his eye that is quite serious. He's also strained a leg muscle, I think. But it looks like he did a lot more damage than was done to him."

"I suppose he had the advantage," said Jane, "being bigger. And also because Ash came into his territory, so Major rightfully defended it tooth and nail."

"Not bad for such an old dog," said Dr. Adam. He came into the room and opened the file. "You know, that dog's nearly thirteen!" He showed Mandy the first page in the file that gave details of Major's birth date, parents, and breeder.

"He's practically the same age as me!" Mandy remarked. "Just a few months older."

"Does that make you very old, too?" teased Dr. Adam, closing the file.

Mandy managed a smile as her dad went out, then watched anxiously as her mom gave Ash an injection. "What's that for?" she asked.

"It's a painkiller and a sedative. It will make him feel much more comfortable for now."

It wasn't long before the collie began to look sleepy. His head drooped and his eyes kept closing.

"I'll go and see how Major's doing," Mandy said, and she went into the neighboring examining room where she found James scrubbing the table. "Where's Major?"

"On the operating table. Your dad's stitching him up," James answered, drying the table with a clean cloth.

Mandy was surprised. "I thought we had to wait for the owners to give their permission."

"We got it," James told her. He peeled off the thick rubber gloves he was wearing. "Sam Western called a few minutes ago and said he might be held up. He didn't want Major to suffer longer than he had to, so he asked your dad to go ahead."

"He must be really worried about him." Mandy sighed. She thought about going into the operating room but changed her mind when she heard a car pulling up outside. "That's probably Andrew Austin. Let's go and meet him."

They went back into the reception area just as Andrew, a tall and burly young man, burst in through the double glass doors. "Where's Ash?" he demanded.

"In here." Mandy pushed open the door to her mom's treatment room.

Dr. Emily and Jane were bending over the dog, but they looked up and nodded to Andrew as he came in.

He looked completely shocked when he saw his dog lying on the table. Dr. Emily was shaving the fur off around all the wounds, ready to stitch them up once Ash was anesthetized.

"Oh, Ash." Andrew sighed. He bent over the collie and stroked his side. "Poor fellow. You must be in agony."

Jane put a comforting hand on his shoulder and said, "He'll be OK. He's in excellent hands."

"Yes, I know," said Andrew. He'd been to Animal Ark before when his mother's dog, an elderly spaniel named Archie, was suffering from bone cancer and had to be put to sleep. "We couldn't have asked for better treatment for Archie when he was here." He looked at Jane and cleared his throat as if he was about to say something, then changed his mind and smoothed Ash's head. "I'm sorry about this, boy," he said softly.

Even though Ash was sedated, he recognized his owner. He blinked and managed to wag the tip of his tail, which brought a lump to Mandy's throat.

"He's pretty out of it right now," Dr. Emily told Andrew, "so he won't be hurting too much." She explained the treatment Ash needed. "He'll have to be kept quiet for a long time when he goes home," she finished, and Mandy guessed that her mom was gently warning Andrew not to let Ash wander again.

"That won't be hard," said Andrew. "He's settled down well. You'd have thought he'd lived on the farm all his life."

Mandy shot James a look. It didn't sound like Ash was a wanderer, so he *must* have been sent out with the card. But to Lydia? Mandy shook her head, and James raised his eyebrows at her, looking just as perplexed. Something didn't add up.

"OK. Let's get Ash taken care of," said Dr. Emily. "Andrew, will you carry him to the operating room, please?"

"Of course." Andrew lifted the collie as if he were a fragile piece of china and followed Dr. Emily and Jane to the operating room.

While the two women worked on the collie, Andrew

waited in the reception area. He said he didn't want to get in the way because there wasn't a lot of space in the operating room. Mandy and James, wanting to help as much as possible, cleaned up Dr. Emily's examining room and were almost finished when they heard angry voices coming from the reception area.

"That sounds like Sam Western arguing with Andrew," said James.

Mandy listened and quickly recognized the two voices as well.

"You'll pay for this, Andrew," Mr. Western was saying. "If anything happens to Major, I'll sue you! I've just seen him, and he's in terrible shape."

"I'm sorry. It was an accident," Andrew replied. "My dog was hurt, too."

"Yes, well, you should keep your dog under control," said Sam. "He could have killed Major."

Mandy had heard enough. She pushed open the door and confronted the angry man who was standing in front of Andrew with his hands on his hips. "And Major could have killed Ash!" she burst out. "He's hurt much worse."

Sam Western took a step back and blinked at Mandy. "Major was defending his territory, so he had every right to attack that collie," he pointed out.

Mandy couldn't argue with this. "He *was* doing his

job," she agreed, "but you can't blame either of the dogs. Sometimes dogs get along" — she paused, thinking of how Blackie and Ash had taken to each other instantly — "and sometimes they're enemies from the word go. It's the way things are in the animal world," James finished behind her.

But Sam Western was not convinced. "That's beside the point," he snapped. "None of this would have happened if Andrew hadn't let that dog stray onto my land."

"I did *not* let him stray," Andrew protested. He started

to pace back and forth. "Look," he said, coming to stand in front of Sam Western again. "I'll gladly pay the vet's bill. But like I said, it was an accident. Ash must have" — he paused and bit his bottom lip — "found a gap in the hedge and gone through. Or even jumped the fence to get into your yard. He's an agile dog, you know."

Andrew's explanation fell on deaf ears. "The vet's bill is not the issue here. It's the agony my dog's in," said Sam Western, and he strode angrily outside.

Andrew stared after him, then shook his head and exhaled. "Uh-oh."

"Don't worry, Andrew," said Mandy. "I'm sure he'll calm down when Major recovers." She guessed that Mr. Western was reacting out of shock. It must have been very upsetting to hear that his dog had been hurt in a fight on his own property. "Come on, James," she said. "We'd better finish cleaning up."

Back in the examining room, Mandy shut the door, then said quietly to James, "You know, I don't think Andrew sent Ash."

James frowned. "Oh, you mean the card," he said. "You think it wasn't from Andrew, after all?"

Mandy nodded as she sprayed disinfectant onto the examination table. "Maybe Ash just took himself out for a walk to explore his new neighborhood and found the envelope lying somewhere, like at the bottom of Lydia's drive."

"Could be," James agreed. He threw some soiled paper towels into the trash can. "Which means that the card was probably not from Andrew, after all. And it might really have been meant for Lydia."

"Well, yes." Mandy put a used syringe into a plastic bag ready to be disposed of properly. "Anyway, that's not really important now." And it was true — all the romantic speculation that morning had been swept away by the terrible drama of the dogfight. In fact, Mandy had almost forgotten that it was Valentine's Day at all.

"The main thing," she said with a sigh, "is that both dogs get well again soon."

Five

"Still feeling awful, Ash?" Mandy murmured, petting the dog through his cage in the residential unit. It was early the next morning, a Sunday, which meant that Mandy could spend the whole day with Ash and Major. She'd woken up even earlier than if it had been a school day and was still in her robe, having wasted no time coming to check on the two dogs and offer them breakfast. They were bound to be hungry after twenty-four hours without food.

The collie lay on a soft sheepskin blanket and stared miserably up at her. It was hard to know if he was missing Andrew, or confused about where he was, or in pain. Probably all three, Mandy thought, petting his shoulder. She put down the bowl of food she'd brought, but Ash didn't even sniff it.

"Oh, dear. No appetite yet," Mandy said. She leaned forward to look closely at the dog's injuries. They somehow seemed worse now that the fur around them had been shaved off. Several rows of black stitches stood out against the bare skin, and more over a wound on Ash's side that Mandy hadn't noticed until after her mom had operated on the dog last night.

"That was a very serious cut," Mandy murmured. She knew that the pipe was to drain off fluid that could cause an infection. "Poor guy," she continued, smoothing Ash's shoulder again. "You thought you'd go for a nice walk to check out your new home, but you ended up causing all sorts of problems and getting yourself all beaten up."

Ash blinked at her. *"I'm sorry,"* he seemed to say.

"You didn't mean to, I know," Mandy said, talking to him as if he really understood her. "But now Andrew's in big trouble with Mr. Western, Major's had to have stitches, too, and Lydia thinks that someone sent her a valentine by dog mail, but it turns out you weren't a maildog after all!"

The collie whined softly and, lifting his head, tried to reach the wound on his side to lick it.

"No. You can't start messing with those stitches," Mandy said, gently pushing his head away. "If you do, Mom will have to put a collar on you." Sometimes when dogs tried to pull out stitches, Mandy's parents had to put stiff plastic collars, like Elizabethan ruffs, around their necks to stop them from being able to reach.

Ash put his head down on the blanket again, but seconds later he looked up and tried to scratch his sewn-up ear with his back leg.

"And don't do that, either," Mandy warned, stopping him by holding his foot. "If nothing else, it'll hurt like crazy if you touch that ear with your sharp nails."

Ash flopped down and sighed, sounding very much like a human who'd had enough of everything.

"You're fed up already, aren't you? I know you'd love to be running across the field," Mandy sympathized, "but you're going to have to wait a while before you can do that again. And when you do, Andrew or someone else will have to go with you. We're not going to have any more fights around here!"

She patted him again, then stood up and went to check on Major. The German shepherd was in a cage at the far end of the residential unit, where the two dogs couldn't see each other.

Before she got to him, there were other patients to feed and fuss over. There was a black-and-white male cat with cystitis, an elderly golden Labrador named Lido who'd had some growths removed from her stomach, and a small Jack Russell terrier who'd been hit by a car that she'd run out to chase. Mandy stopped at each cage and put a dish of food inside, while talking softly to the patient.

"I think you're going home today, Eddie," she said to the cat. Eddie was rather unfriendly and had dived under his bedding to hide. "I know you're there." She chuckled, patting the lump under the blanket.

She moved on to the Jack Russell, whose back legs were heavily bandaged. "Lucky for you, nothing was broken," Mandy said, scratching the little dog between her ears. "But next time, it could be different. If I were you, I'd think twice about chasing cars again."

Before going to Lido's cage, she glanced back at Eddie's and saw his big yellow eyes peeping out from under the blanket. "Be brave," Mandy told him. "Come out and face the big wide world."

Eddie did exactly the opposite and disappeared under the covers again.

Mandy shrugged and went to visit Lido. The yellow Labrador was delighted to have a visitor. She whined with pleasure and wagged her tail when Mandy crouched down in front of her. "You're doing well, Lido," she remarked. "You might even go home today."

She patted the friendly animal before finally going to Major's cage.

Mandy was surprised to find that he was fast asleep. "Still sleeping off the anesthetic?" she whispered as she quietly put his food in the cage. She sat and observed Major for a few minutes, hoping he would sense her presence and wake up. But he stayed asleep, his legs twitching every now and then as he dreamed.

"At least you look peaceful," Mandy murmured. She

waited with him a little longer, then decided to go back upstairs to get dressed. "Be back soon," she said softly as she left the unit.

Ten minutes later she returned, eating a slice of toast that she'd grabbed on her way through the kitchen. But this time she wasn't the only one checking the patients. Her mom was there, too, examining Major's stitches.

"Morning, dear," Dr. Emily said, glancing over her shoulder at Mandy.

"Morning, Mom." Mandy saw that Major was wide awake and that his food bowl was empty. "Well, hi there," she said, kneeling down. "I see you haven't lost your appetite."

Major put his head to one side as if trying to figure out what she was saying.

"You must be feeling a lot better," Mandy continued, and Major put his head on the other side.

Mandy laughed and smoothed the fur between his upright ears. "Typical German shepherd, following the conversation when someone talks to you!"

Dr. Emily seemed satisfied with Major's progress. "A few more days and no one will know you've been in a fight," she said as she closed the door to his cage. "Let's have a look at Ash now and see if he's doing just as well."

"He was restless when I saw him earlier, and not at all hungry," Mandy told her mom as they approached the collie's cage.

Ash gazed up at them as they bent down in front of him. Then he dropped his head between his front paws and half closed his eyes.

"Not a happy boy," Dr. Emily agreed, opening the cage. She pushed aside the untouched bowl of food, then examined Ash's wounds, gently pressing the skin next to the stitches. "So far, so good," she said, but when she came to the wound on the collie's ear, she frowned. "Mmm. It's quite inflamed."

"No wonder he's so miserable," Mandy pointed out.

Dr. Emily reached for a thermometer in the pocket of her white coat and took Ash's temperature. "Oh, dear," she said when she saw what it was. "It looks like Ash has picked up an infection."

Mandy looked closely. The mercury was at 103 degrees — about two degrees more than a dog's normal temperature. Ash had to be feeling terrible!

"We'd better get some antibiotics into him immediately," said Dr. Emily. She hurried out and returned a few minutes later with a syringe. "I was going to start him on a course of pills today," she continued, gently pinching some loose skin on his neck before injecting the drug. "But this infection needs more aggressive treatment." She withdrew the needle and massaged the spot where it had gone in.

Ash blinked up at Mandy and her mom, trying to focus on them.

"I know you hurt all over and you're feeling terrible," Mandy said soothingly. She ran her hand through his silky coat. "But we're going to do everything we can to make sure you get better." Mandy had full faith in her mom's ability to treat the dog, but deep down, she felt anything but confident. Ash seemed a lot worse than he'd been yesterday. *Just how bad is the infection?* Mandy wondered. *What if it's spread farther than his ear?* Her mind started to race and the word *septicemia* sprang to mind. *If Ash develops blood poisoning . . .* The consequences were too painful to think about, so Mandy blocked the thought by telling herself that everything would be fine. At least they'd caught the infection early.

Dr. Emily had been checking the rest of Ash's injuries to be certain none of the others had become infected, too. Now she glanced at her watch. "I have some calls to make. Are you staying here, Mandy?"

"Definitely," Mandy said. "I'll give everyone some clean water, then sit with Ash for a while."

"Thanks, honey," said Dr. Emily, going to the door. "But don't spend all day in here. Make sure you go out for some fresh air."

"OK," Mandy said. Going out was the last thing on her mind. She'd gladly sit with Ash all day if it helped him feel better. She thought of Andrew. He'd probably want to keep his beloved dog company, as well. "Someone's got to tell Andrew," she called after her mom, who glanced back and said, "Yes, I was about to do that."

Mandy stroked the listless collie. "Poor Ash," she murmured. "And poor Andrew. He's worried enough about you, so it's going to be a big blow when he hears you have an infection. And on top of that, he's in trouble with his boss. But Mr. Western might be a bit more understanding when he hears how sick you are, Ash."

As she smoothed the collie's soft, shining coat, Mandy thought how beautiful he still looked, despite his condition. Things couldn't have turned out worse. *So much for a happy Valentine's Day*, she mused gloomily.

Six

Mandy changed the water in the patients' bowls and even managed to get a purr out of Eddie. Although the cat stayed under his bedding, she smoothed his hunched-up back until she felt the telltale vibration. "That's better," she said, smiling. "We'll be friends before you leave here, you'll see."

"Friends with whom?" asked James, coming in just then. Amy was behind him; Mandy guessed they must have met up on their way to Animal Ark.

After the dogs had come out of the operating room yesterday, Mandy had phoned High Cross Farm to tell Lydia and Amy what had happened. They'd both been

65

horrified to hear the news, and Amy had wanted to come right over to see the dogs, but it was late. Lydia had told her she'd have to wait till morning when she could ride down to the village.

"Is it OK if we come in?" Amy whispered, as if she was in a hospital.

"Sure," Mandy said, beckoning them over to the collie's cage. "He's feeling pretty sick," she explained. "That wound on his ear's infected."

Amy peered in at Ash who was now asleep. "He's hurt so badly!" She gasped, her eyes wide. "It must have been a terrible fight. But he didn't seem aggressive when he was at Aunt Lydia's yesterday. I mean, remember how well he and Blackie got along?"

"Yes, but that might have been because both of them were on neutral territory," said James.

"Probably," Mandy agreed. She took them over to Major who saw them coming and started to get up, but flopped down again as if it was too much trouble to stand.

Mandy petted him through the wire. "Don't worry, boy. You're just a bit wobbly after the anesthetic."

The German shepherd licked Mandy's hand, then wagged his tail as James crouched down and petted him, too. "Good thing your dad was there when the fight happened," James told Mandy. "It would have been a disaster otherwise."

Just then, Simon popped his head around the door. Even though Sunday was usually his day off, he'd come in to lend a hand with the extra patients. "Is everything OK?" he asked.

Mandy nodded.

"In that case, your mom says you can take a break," he told her. "She wants you to go up to Lilac Cottage to get some fresh vegetables from your grandpa."

Mandy didn't want to leave Ash and Major. "What if one of the dogs needs us?"

"They'll be fine," Simon reassured her. "Jane's coming over after lunch. It's her day off, too, but she promised to help out. And your dad will be back in about ten minutes." Dr. Adam had been called out earlier to help with a difficult triple lambing.

Determined to get the vegetables and come right back to Animal Ark, Mandy set off with James and Amy. They took their bikes for the short ride to Lilac Cottage.

"Hello, there! Oh, and Amy, how nice to see you, too," Grandma Hope called out the kitchen window when she saw the three friends leaning their bicycles against the hedge. "You're just in time for some fresh muffins."

"Great!" called James. At the same time, Mandy said,

"We're not staying. We have to get back to Ash and Major."

"Ash and Major?" Grandpa echoed, coming across from his greenhouse with a wicker basket full of vegetables.

"Two patients in the residential unit," Mandy explained. She followed her grandfather inside where she told him and Gran about the dogfight.

Grandpa listened while he put some of the vegetables into a shopping bag. "A dogfight's a frightening thing to see," he remarked when Mandy had finished. "But it could have been worse."

"Much worse," Mandy agreed. She took the bag from him. "Thanks, Grandpa. We'll be going now."

"Hold on a minute," said Grandpa Hope. "You're staying for a morning snack, aren't you?"

"Yes, please," said James and Amy, their combined voices stifling Mandy's "no."

"Of course they are," said Gran. She put an arm around Mandy. "I think those dogs will survive without you for a short while."

"But someone needs to keep an eye on them," Mandy protested.

"Your mom and dad are doing that," said Gran. She took her arm from around Mandy's shoulder and said in a serious tone, "You have to learn to step back from your patients if you're going to be a vet. If you get emotionally involved with every animal you treat, you'll turn into a nervous wreck."

Mandy knew her grandmother was right. It was something her mom and dad had told her often, too. "You have to try to distance yourself from the situation sometimes," they were always reminding her. But how could anyone be objective when an animal was suffering?

Mandy shrugged. "OK. We'll have some milk and muffins." She saw James smile at Amy, who took off her red jacket and put it on the back of a chair.

"You're in for a treat," he told her. "Mandy's grandmother is the best baker in Welford."

"That's what Aunt Lydia says," said Amy. She noticed a tray of freshly baked golden muffins on the kitchen counter. "Those look delicious."

"They are. But we're not going to stay long," Mandy warned. "Just one each, and then we're out of here."

Gran went to pour the milk but Grandpa stopped her. "I'm chief cook and bottle washer around here for a day or two, remember?" he said with a warm smile. "So I'll get the milk and butter the muffins." He took the pitcher from Gran, then put it down and clapped his hands together, sending everyone out of the kitchen.

"What was all that about?" Mandy asked Gran when they were in the living room.

Gran chuckled and pointed to a vase of red roses and a valentine card on the coffee table. "That's what it's about," she said. "Your grandpa's gotten sentimental lately. Just like when we were courting all those years ago."

"Not him, too!" James sighed, looking thoroughly fed up with the idea of romance. "Everyone's gone mushy."

Gran chuckled. "You'll change your tune in a few years' time."

"Never!" retorted James.

Amy was as enthusiastic as ever about anything to do with Valentine's Day. "Red roses! That's so romantic. And a heart-shaped card, too!"

"But Valentine's Day was yesterday," James protested.

"So?" said Amy. "That doesn't mean people have to stop being romantic and throw away their flowers and cards. I even saw Aunt Lydia peeping at her card again this morning."

"Lydia got a card? Who sent it?" asked Gran, rearranging a couple of the roses.

Mandy had flopped down on the sofa. "We don't know," she said. "Ash just appeared with it."

Gran looked surprised. She stopped what she was doing, and, holding one of the roses, turned and looked at Mandy. "But didn't you say Ash belongs to Andrew Austin?"

"Yes."

"Then that means he must have sent the card," said Gran.

"Impossible," James blurted out. His eyes lit up as Grandpa came in carrying a plate of muffins, thickly spread with strawberry jam and butter. "Yum!" he said.

"Why is it impossible?" asked Gran, moving the vase to make space for the plate.

James didn't take his eyes off the plate. "Because Andrew's a lot younger than Lydia."

"Well, I hope it *was* Andrew," Amy said dreamily. She sat cross-legged on the floor in front of the roses and gazed at the flowers, resting her chin in her hands. "That would be so romantic."

James made a face at her.

Realizing she was hungry after having had only one slice of toast for breakfast, Mandy leaned forward and helped herself to a muffin. "Sorry to disappoint you both," she told her two friends, "but we can't even be sure that the card was for Lydia in the first place. It could have blown out of someone's mailbox or car window, or one of the neighbors might have lost it. It could have even been meant for Mr. Western, seeing as he's next door to Lydia."

James was about to sink his teeth into a muffin, but he quickly took it out of his mouth. "No way! I mean, can you imagine Sam Western having a secret admirer? He's much too bad-tempered."

Mandy almost agreed with him, but then she remembered how upset Sam had been over Major. "That's not exactly true," she admitted. "Think of how much he loves Major."

"That's different," said James. "I was talking about humans."

Gran gave him a sideways glance. "Sam Western might not be everyone's favorite uncle, but that doesn't give you the right to speak badly of him."

"Sorry," said James, looking a bit sheepish. "It's just that . . ." He trailed off, unable to think of what to say.

"It's just that you haven't often seen him in a good light," suggested Grandpa, coming in with a pitcher of milk and some glasses.

"That's probably it," Mandy agreed, getting up to help her grandfather. She took the glasses off the tray and set them on the coffee table. "We know he can be very stern, but deep down, there must be some good in him."

Mandy found herself thinking about Sam Western again after lunch the next day. It was the start of the midterm school vacation, and she was cleaning out the cages in the residential unit. Her parents had gone to a veterinary meeting in Walton, and Mandy had offered to keep an eye on Ash and Major. They were the only patients left — the others had gone home earlier that day.

"You've probably seen a side of your master that no one else has," Mandy said, trying to ease Major's blanket out from under him so she could replace it with a clean one. But even though she tugged at the blanket, the German shepherd wouldn't move off it. He gazed at her with his big, almond-shaped eyes that, once so bright and clear, were now clouded by cataracts. Mandy had often seen milky films like this over the eyes of elderly dogs and knew that they would eventually take Major's sight away altogether.

"But not just yet," she murmured, playing with his ears. "Come on, old boy," she urged him. "You'll have to stand up. I can't get this blanket out from under you." She took him by the collar and gently pulled him toward her. "And anyway, Mom and Dad think it's time you had a bit of exercise. Even Ash has been out for a sniff around the garden this morning, and he's in much worse shape than you."

There was no doubt that Ash had come in second in the fight, especially after developing the infection. But Mandy thought, or maybe she just hoped, that he seemed slightly better this morning. He'd had a few mouthfuls of food and come out of his cage to limp beside Mandy to the exercise track outside. He'd walked around slowly for a few minutes before flopping down on the ground as if the little bit of exercise had exhausted him.

"Come on, Major," Mandy urged again, trying to get the old dog to stand up.

Reluctantly, Major pulled himself up and took a few steps forward before collapsing on the floor of his cage, his face twisted in pain.

Mandy's heart skipped a beat. "You're still hurting!" she cried. "That's why you didn't want to get up." She checked his wounds, desperately hoping they hadn't opened up or that her dad hadn't missed one when he'd patched the dog up the other night. But they all looked clean and were healing well.

"What's the matter?" she wondered out loud, feeling Major all over, in case his thick coat was concealing something.

Major gazed trustingly at her and licked her hand when she brought it up to his handsome head. Mandy remembered her dad saying the dog might have pulled a leg muscle in the fight. She felt his forelegs, then gently touched the muscles in his upper legs, but Major didn't even flinch.

"That can't be the problem," she said. She checked his paws, thinking that something like a stone or a thorn could be lodged in the tender pads. But once again, she drew a blank. "It might have been a cramp," she murmured, pulling at straws in hopes that there was nothing seriously wrong with Major. "Let's try again," she said and, clapping her hands encouragingly, she tried to entice him out of his cage. "Come on, Major. Let's go for a walk."

The old dog sighed and, trying his hardest to please Mandy, rose awkwardly to his feet. He only managed to hobble forward a few steps, before his back legs buckled and he slumped to the floor.

Mandy was certain now that Major was in serious trouble. "You poor boy," she said, crouching beside him and putting her arms around his neck. "I'll phone Mom and Dad and get them to come home right away." Her voice was choked with emotion. She didn't care if her Gran thought she got too involved — she just couldn't bear seeing an animal in pain.

She ran into the reception area where she grabbed the phone book and flipped through the pages until she found the name of the place where the meeting was being held. She punched in the number listed alongside it. "Hurry up. Answer the phone!" she muttered, listening to the ringing. She waited for what seemed like ages, but no one answered. She slammed down the receiver in frustration. Then Mandy remembered that her dad would probably have his cell phone with him. She dialed the number. Again there was no answer other than a recorded voice saying that her dad was unavailable and that she could leave a message. He must have switched off his phone or left it in the car.

"Dad, there's something terribly wrong with Major," Mandy said into the phone. "Please come home as soon as you get this message."

She hung up, feeling utterly helpless. The old dog was in tremendous pain, but all alone, Mandy could do nothing. She certainly couldn't start dishing painkillers out to him. All she could do was to sit with him and try to comfort him.

Just then, she heard someone tapping on the front door and calling her name.

"Jane!" Mandy cried with relief when she recognized the voice. She spun around and ran to let her in, then saw that Andrew was there, too. "Am I glad to see you!" Mandy told them.

"Nice to get a friendly welcome," said Jane, smiling. "Andrew and I bumped into each other outside the Fox and Goose on our way here."

"Is it OK for us to see Ash?" asked Andrew. He'd come over yesterday after he'd heard about the infection. Mandy had been at Lilac Cottage with James and Amy at the time, but Simon had told her that Andrew was devastated to find Ash looking worse than before.

He'd promised to come back today as soon as he'd finished his work on the farm.

"Oh, sure. It's fine," Mandy said, then burst out, "but Major's in a lot of trouble and I don't know what to do!" She was on the verge of tears, either out of sheer relief that someone with at least *some* veterinary knowledge had arrived or because she was so desperately worried about the German shepherd. She swallowed hard before telling Jane what had happened and that she couldn't get hold of her parents. "But you can check Major, can't you?" she finished.

"I'm not sure I'll be able to help much," Jane warned as they went into the residential unit. "In fact, you probably know more about animals than I do."

The old dog thumped his tail when he saw them. There was a look of trust in his dark brown eyes as if he was sure they'd come to help him.

Mandy knelt down in front of him. "Jane's here to take a look at you."

"You don't need me getting in the way, so I'll go and sit with Ash," said Andrew, leaving them with a worried glance at the German shepherd.

"You say Major collapsed when he tried to get up?" asked Jane, kneeling down.

"Yes. It's like he can't take his own weight," Mandy explained.

Jane examined Major's legs, but the German shepherd showed no sign of any distress. "Well, it can't be anything like serious bruising or a broken leg," said Jane. "Unless it's not his legs at all."

"If it's not his legs, then what —" Mandy stopped as a thought flashed through her mind. "Perhaps it has nothing to do with him being hurt in the fight," she said slowly.

"It could be an old injury that's suddenly flared up again," Jane agreed. "Or even arthritis, which would make his joints ache like crazy, especially after he's been lying down for a couple of days."

"Joint pain?" Mandy pictured the shelves full of veterinary science books in her mom and dad's examining rooms. "Come on, let's see what we can find out."

Leaving Andrew with Ash, she and Jane went to read up on the subject. Mandy took a thick reference book down from one of the shelves and flipped through it. She soon came to a chapter dealing with joint problems. There were several subsections, each one describing a different condition. With Jane leaning over her shoulder, she glanced through the various topics. "It could be arthritis," she murmured, reading the symptoms for the disease before quickly scanning the next paragraph, which dealt with sudden injury.

"It could also be trauma, from the fight," said Jane, reading the same section.

Mandy had already finished that paragraph and was reading the next. Suddenly, the answer hit her like a thunderbolt.

"Hip dysplasia!" she declared, her heart skipping a beat as the two words jumped out from the page. "That's got to be it! It says here it's very common in German shepherds. If Major's hips don't fit properly in their sockets, he can't even stand, let alone walk."

Seven

X-rays of Major's hips confirmed Mandy's diagnosis.

"Classic hip dysplasia," announced Dr. Emily, holding up the X-ray in front of a light.

When Dr. Adam had heard Mandy's desperate message, he and her mother had rushed back to Animal Ark. Andrew was still there, and he had helped Dr. Adam carry Major into an examining room and place him carefully on the table. Dr. Emily had sedated the dog so that he would lie still for the X-ray.

Now, fifteen minutes later, the terrible truth was clearly visible.

"Major's hips are in a terrible state," continued Dr.

Emily. She outlined the hip joints with her index finger. "You can see how the ball joints don't fit inside the sockets."

"But you can treat him, can't you?" Mandy asked her mom. She was standing next to the sleeping dog, stroking his noble head.

Dr. Emily exchanged a glance with her husband before looking back at Mandy. "We'll do everything we can," she promised.

"Starting right now," said Dr. Adam. He filled a syringe with the contents of a small ampoule. "We'll give him an anti-inflammatory shot first." He injected Major, then he and Andrew carried the dog back to the residential unit.

Mandy went with them and put two thick sheepskin rugs in the cage to make sure Major had an extra-soft bed. "See you later," she whispered to the drowsy dog when she stood up to leave.

On the way out, Mandy, her dad, and Andrew paused to check on Ash. The collie was asleep. When Dr. Adam felt his good ear he said, "It feels pretty warm. He's still got a raging temperature."

Andrew said nothing, but the look on his face told Mandy just how worried he was.

Back in the reception area they came face-to-face with Sam Western.

He must have practically flown here, Mandy thought. Her mom had called Mr. Western as soon as the X-rays confirmed the diagnosis, and even though he was busy in the dairy he'd come over right away.

"I need to see my dog," Sam Western told Dr. Adam, pushing past him and going into the residential unit.

"He's in the cage at the end," Mandy called, and she ran after him to show him.

Even though he was still sedated, Major seemed to know that Mr. Western was there. He lifted his head and blinked, then thumped his tail slowly on the sheepskin rug.

Sam Western crouched down and stroked his dog's head. "OK, boy," he murmured. His voice was hoarse and had lost all its brusqueness. It sounded as if, like Mandy, he was choking back tears. "Take it easy, old fellow. You rest, and I'll see to it that you get all the treatment you need." He continued smoothing Major's fur for a few minutes. Then, when the dog's eyes began to droop, he stood up and went out of the unit, passing Ash on the way. He paused to look at the collie. "He's not looking too good, either," he remarked.

"No. He's got a serious infection," Mandy said.

Mandy's mom and Jane had joined Dr. Adam and Andrew in the waiting room.

"I'm so sorry about Major," Dr. Emily said to Mr.

Western. She held up the X-rays. "Do you want to look at these?"

"No. I'll take your word for it. You're the expert," said Sam Western. He turned to Andrew. "I see Ash has also taken a turn for the worse."

Andrew sighed. "Yes. I suppose we're in a similar boat, you and I."

"Of course, this wouldn't have happened to Major if your dog hadn't attacked him," remarked Mr. Western.

Andrew looked taken aback. "Sorry?" he said, frowning. But he collected himself quickly and said, "Now just hold it right there, Sam. You can't pin this on my dog."

"Ash had nothing to do with it," Jane confirmed, backing Andrew up.

"Oh, but he did. There was nothing wrong with Major before the fight," Sam Western insisted.

"How do you know?" Mandy blurted out.

Before the argument could develop, Dr. Emily stepped forward. "Andrew and Jane are right, Mr. Western. You can't blame Ash for Major's condition. Hip dysplasia is a congenital disease. Major's had it all his life."

"Impossible!" blustered Mr. Western.

"Not impossible," said Dr. Emily. "He's coped well until now, and that's probably why you didn't realize he had a problem. But with him getting older, the condition is becoming more marked. You must have noticed him getting slower. Perhaps even battling to get up sometimes?"

Sam Western sighed and looked out the window. He was silent for a moment, then, still staring straight ahead, he said, "I suppose he has been slower recently. And I thought his back legs were a bit weak, but I told myself I was just imagining things."

"You weren't," Dr. Emily said softly, going to stand next to him.

"He seemed a bit wobbly when I saw him for the first time the other day," put in Jane.

But Sam Western wasn't convinced that Major's sudden decline was unrelated to the fight. He looked around at Andrew again. "I still say it's your dog's fault. Major was getting around just fine until Ash strayed onto my property and attacked him. Now he can't even stand."

Andrew had no answer to the accusation. "I'm really sorry," he began, looking upset.

But while Mandy realized that Mr. Western had a point, she was also certain that the fight had played only a small role. "It's not fair to blame Ash. It was just unlucky," she insisted. "Major's probably been careful for a long time about how much activity he does because his hips have been hurting. But the fight made him forget, and now he's in agony. Maybe jumping around like that made the hip dysplasia worse."

Dr. Adam nodded in agreement. "That just about sums it up," he said. "The fight might have played a role, but only in that it brought the underlying problem to the surface. Major might have gone on for another few weeks, even a couple of months, before he got to this point. It didn't necessarily have to be something as dramatic as a fight. Just a fall or a knock could have done the trick, too."

Sam Western sat down heavily in a chair, as if the news had finally sunk in. He rested his head in his hands and stared at the floor.

"Of course, we'll do all we can to help Major," Dr. Emily told him.

Mr. Western looked up again. "It's hard to see an animal you love having such a rough time," he said quietly.

For the first time since she'd known the man, Mandy felt a sharp pang of sympathy for him. "It's the worst thing," she agreed, then repeated what her mom had said earlier. "But Mom and Dad will make sure he doesn't suffer."

"We'll do everything we can for him," Dr. Emily confirmed. "I might even try acupuncture to ease the pain." She had studied the technique during a trip to China.

"And surgery?" asked Mr. Western, getting up. "I don't care what it costs, you know. If he needs it, he'll have it."

Dr. Adam looked at him and sighed. "We'll have to think about that."

But five minutes later, after everyone had left, Dr. Adam confided in Mandy and her mom. "I think we might have raised Sam's hopes too high."

"You mean about him not feeling a lot of pain?" Mandy asked, looking over her shoulder at her dad. She'd put the X-rays in Major's file, which she was returning to the drawer next to Jean's desk.

Dr. Adam seemed reluctant to answer. "Not just that," he said, running his hand through his hair. "You're not going to like this, Mandy."

"Like what?" Mandy's heart started to beat faster.

"I'm really sorry, honey, but surgery's not the answer for Major."

"Then what is?"

Her mom looked very serious. "Unfortunately, there is no answer for advanced hip dysplasia, other than to keep Major as free of pain as we can. And there's no guarantee how long our treatment will work, if at all."

"Are you saying that there's absolutely nothing you can do to make him better?" Mandy demanded.

Her parents looked at her sadly. "I'm afraid not," answered Dr. Emily.

Eight

"Mandy! You're putting hand lotion in the cheese molds!" Amy's voice cut into Mandy's thoughts, bringing her back to the present — in the kitchen at High Cross Farm a day later.

With the order books overflowing and the midterm break coming along at just the right time, Mandy and James were helping Lydia and Amy pack heart-shaped cheeses and bottles of hand lotion, both made from goat's milk, into straw-lined baskets. Even though Valentine's Day had passed, there was still a big demand for the products that Lydia had mentioned in her radio interview. The heart-shaped cheese had been Amy's idea, and Mandy had suggested packaging it into gift baskets along with the hand lotion.

"Yikes!" Mandy exclaimed when Amy's timely warning made her realize what she'd been doing. Instead of putting the soft white cheese into the heart-shaped molds, she'd poured creamy lotion into them.

"Whoa, Mandy! You're really out of it today," remarked James, who was lining the little square baskets with straw. He wasn't just talking about the mistake with the hand lotion. Mandy had ridden right past him at the intersection outside the Fox and Goose where they'd arranged to meet that morning. He'd had to race after her bike, calling her name, before she noticed him. "What's on your mind, Mandy?"

"Major. And Ash, of course," Mandy said, trying to tip the lotion back out of the molds into a jug. Before coming up to the farm that morning, she had spent about half an hour with the two dogs. Ash hadn't responded to the medication as well as Dr. Emily had expected. He was obviously in a lot of pain and was hardly eating.

Major still had his appetite, but he wouldn't stand and had to eat lying down. And then there was the complication of taking him outside so he could relieve himself. Early that morning, Mandy and her dad had carried him out to the track where the brave old dog had struggled to stay on his feet. He'd tried to support himself with his front legs alone, but after a few minutes, even with Mandy holding him around his middle, he had given up and flopped down onto the damp grass.

"Mom's giving Major acupuncture this morning," Mandy told James and Amy. "So keep your fingers crossed that it helps. Dad says he can't keep giving him anti-inflammatories."

Lydia had come in while Mandy was speaking. "That's an unusual idea, Mandy," she said, looking at the lotion-filled molds. "Heart-shaped hand lotion."

Mandy started to explain, feeling rather embarrassed, but Lydia stopped her. "It's hard to concentrate when you're worrying about an animal," she said. Of all people, Lydia knew what it was like to be in that position. Her goat, Houdini, had been at death's door after he'd eaten the rhododendron bush, and although Lydia had tried to put up a brave front, Mandy had known that deep down, she was beside herself with worry.

"It'll be easier to scrape the lotion out of those molds with a spoon," Lydia continued. She took one out of a drawer and gave it to Mandy.

The phone rang and Lydia picked up the cordless receiver. Despite being preoccupied with Major and Ash, Mandy smiled as she watched Lydia press the button to speak to the caller. Not so long ago, Lydia hadn't even owned a phone, let alone a cordless one. The only modern conveniences in her ancient cottage had been running water and electricity, and she still had no television or radio. But once people started to order her goat's milk, Lydia had agreed that she needed a phone. Just lately, she'd switched to a cordless one so she could take orders even when she was in the barn or out in the pastures.

"High Cross Farm," Lydia said in a voice that Mandy hardly recognized. It seemed that Lydia still felt rather self-conscious when she spoke on the phone.

"Fifteen cheese hearts and lotions," Lydia said, making a note of the order. "I'll get those out to you as soon as I can. Perhaps even later today." She pressed the OFF button on the receiver and put it on the dresser. "That was Walton Natural Products," she said, looking very pleased. "It's their second order this week."

"You'll be a millionaire soon at this rate," joked James.

"And pigs will fly," said Lydia, chuckling.

Mandy took the cheese molds to the sink. As she rinsed them out in hot soapy water, she looked out the window at Houdini and the other goats. They'd always been in good condition, but now they looked better than ever. Their coats were thick and glossy, and their bodies strong and well fed.

On the far side of the pasture was the stretch of

moorland where Mandy had first seen Ash. She pictured the sleek brown-and-white dog running easily over the grass, but as she stared, another sight came into view: a battered old van bumping up to the cottage. "I think you have a visitor," she told Lydia.

Lydia frowned and clicked her tongue. "Who is it now, I wonder?" She sounded impatient, but Mandy knew this was just a front. Lydia wasn't really unfriendly, just shy and a little awkward around people.

"It's Ernie Bell," Mandy said, recognizing the van. This wasn't difficult because no one else in Welford, or the whole of Walton for that matter, drove anything like Ernie's van. Once a shiny bright blue, it was now dull and faded, with dents on the fenders and in both front doors. In place of the window on the passenger's side, there was a sheet of crumpled plastic that Ernie had taped to the frame. Mandy had once gotten up the courage to ask him why he didn't get a new window, and Ernie had simply said there was no need. The plastic worked as well as glass, and at least it wouldn't shatter!

People can be so stubborn, Mandy told herself as she watched the retired carpenter stop the van in front of the cottage before climbing out with a toolbox in one hand.

Lydia looked out the window beside Mandy. "Oh, he's

come to fix a section of Houdini's fence," she said. "He promised he'd come and do it when he had the chance." She quickly took off the stained apron she was wearing and patted down her hair, then put the kettle on the stove to boil. "But he could have called to let me know he was coming this morning," she added, sounding rather flustered.

Mandy was sure that Lydia's cheeks had turned pink. Was she embarrassed to have a sudden visitor? Or was it just the warmth from the old coal stove that was making her blush?

Ernie clambered up to the kitchen door in his sturdy black boots. Amy opened it for him, and he peered in at Lydia. "I don't want to bother you," he said gruffly. "I've just come to mend that part of the fence."

"So you won't come in for tea, then?" asked Lydia.

Ernie looked past her at the kettle. "I never said that," he replied, his forehead creased into its usual frown.

"Well, you can't have it there, standing on the back step," said Lydia, as if scolding him. "Come on in."

Ernie looked down at his boots. "I'll have to take these off."

"No, you don't. They're not muddy," replied Lydia.

Walking on tiptoe in case some dirt was clinging to the soles of his boots, Ernie went to sit down at the table. He took off his cap and put it on his lap, then seemed to notice for the first time what Mandy and the others were doing. "Busy, aren't you?" he commented, looking at the bottles of hand lotion and the molds of cheese.

"Yep. The more we pack, the more the orders come in," said James, and he counted the baskets. "Still about fifteen short," he said to Lydia, who was spooning tea leaves into a cracked china teapot.

"Don't they look pretty?" Mandy said, picking up one of the baskets and offering it to Ernie.

The man recoiled as if she'd offered him a snake. "I won't be taking one," he said at once.

"I don't think Mandy's asking you to," said Lydia, pouring boiling water into the teapot.

"I was only asking you what you thought of it," Mandy confirmed.

Ernie shrugged. "I suppose it's all right, if you like that kind of thing."

Amy looked insulted. After all, the heart-shaped cheese was her idea. "Well, lots of people do, Mr. Bell. And Aunt Lydia's going to make a lot of money out of all this."

"In that case, she'd better get some more goats. Like the herd George Cartwright offered to sell her." Ernie stared into his cup as Lydia poured tea into it. "And concentrate on selling milk rather than peddling trinkets."

"They're not trinkets," Amy protested. "They're very nice presents."

Lydia raised the teapot, and with her other hand on her hip, she looked down at Ernie. "How did you know about Mr. Cartwright offering me his goats?"

Ernie raised his bushy white eyebrows with a glimmer of a smile. "Well, you know what they say about living in a small town, don't you?"

"No, I don't," Lydia said sternly. "What do they say?"

"If you don't know what you're doing, at least everyone else does." Ernie stopped smiling. "And I'm serious. If you turn down those goats, you'll be making a big mistake."

Lydia looked as if she wanted to break the teapot over his head. "Are you calling me a fool?" she wanted to know.

"I didn't say so. But now that you mention it, yes, you're a fool not to have accepted George's offer. You'll probably never get such a good chance again."

Amy's eyes stretched wide, and Mandy could see that she was taken aback by Ernie's abruptness. She wanted to tell Amy that it was just an act and that, deep down, Ernie Bell had a heart of gold. But now was not the time.

Lydia set the teapot down so hard that the lid rattled. "You might have put up the new fence for me, Ernie

Bell, but that doesn't give you the right to tell me how I should run my business."

"I'm only giving you my opinion," responded Ernie. He put three teaspoons of sugar into his cup and stirred it. The clinking of the spoon was the only sound for a few seconds before he spoke again. "And it's my opinion that you need to move with the times."

"Move with the times!" Lydia echoed. "That's something, coming from you." She looked out the window at Ernie's ancient van. "Move with the times, indeed," she muttered again, shaking her head.

Mandy caught James's eye, then looked away quickly. If she hadn't, she'd have burst out laughing. Ernie and Lydia were like a comic act. At the same time, though, she was puzzled. Ernie seemed to be showing a lot more than just a friendly interest in Lydia's business.

But he is famous for arguing about everything, Mandy reminded herself. Perhaps that was why he'd opposed Lydia's view about Mr. Cartwright's offer.

Back at Animal Ark later that day, Mandy and James were making sure Ash and Major were comfortable for the night when Andrew arrived with his mother to visit his dog.

It was the first time Mrs. Austin had seen Ash since

the fight, and she was shocked at the sight of his injuries. "That ear looks very damaged," she said, clasp-
ing her hands to her chest. "The other dog must be very
strong to have done that."

"He's not strong anymore," Mandy said sadly.

Mrs. Austin shook her head. "I suppose not. Andrew
told me about the hip problem. What a shame that an
old dog should be in so much pain." A shadow crossed
her face, and Mandy guessed she was thinking of her
spaniel, Archie. Mrs. Austin had been devastated when
she lost her faithful companion, but the family of feral
cats that she'd taken in had helped to console her.

"Do you want to see Major?" Mandy asked.

"Yes, please," said Mrs. Austin.

The German shepherd tried to get up when he saw
them. He managed to heave himself up into a sitting position and licked Mandy's hand when she put it through
the wire to pet him.

"That's a good boy," Mandy said.

James had been peering into the cage to see if he
could detect some change in the dog. "Do you think he
looks a little better after the acupuncture?"

"Acupuncture?" Mrs. Austin echoed, also putting her
hand through the wire mesh to pet Major.

"Yes. Mom says it could help with the pain," Mandy explained. "And it does look like he's feeling a little better. Mom and Jane gave him his first treatment this morning."

"Is that the same Jane who came over with Andrew to meet the cats the other day?" said Mrs. Austin.

"Yep," said Andrew, coming over to Major's cage and bending down to pet him, too. "She's been helping out here." He glanced around, then said casually to Mandy, "She's not still here by any chance, is she?"

Mandy shook her head, and Andrew said, "Well, I guess we'll bump into her another time. Especially since Ash is probably going to be here for a while."

"Or you could ask her to come and visit again," suggested Mrs. Austin. "She was wonderful with Cinders and the kittens."

"Yeah. Well, maybe," said Andrew. "But she's probably too busy at the farm."

"No, she's not." James stood up straight. "She was still here when Mandy and I got back from Lydia's at lunchtime, and she said she was glad that her schedule allows her so much time off. She really likes coming to help out at Animal Ark. She and Simon get along well."

James's remark seemed to make Andrew uncomfortable. "Well, we'll see," was his terse comment, and Mandy was sure she saw him blush before he turned and went back to Ash's cage.

But it wasn't until after the Austins had left that

Mandy figured out what might lie behind Andrew's un-expected reaction.

"That's it!" she cried, a light going on in her head at the same time she was switching off the one in the residential unit. It was early evening and the clinic was closed. Mandy and James were the last to leave and were making sure everything was locked up for the night.

James frowned at her. "What's what?"

"The card! Andrew sent it," Mandy declared.

"The one Lydia got?"

"Of course."

James stopped and folded his arms. "But we've been through all this before, and we decided Andrew couldn't have sent Lydia the card."

"That's not what I mean, silly," Mandy said, which made James look even more puzzled.

"Then what?"

Mandy locked the door to the reception area and led the way through to the kitchen. "Ash was probably delivering the card after all."

"Honestly, Mandy," said James. "You must be dreaming if you think Andrew wanted to send a valentine to Lydia."

"I'm not saying that at all. But I really do think Ash was being a maildog." Mandy opened the fridge to take out a couple of sodas and handed one to James.

He flicked back the tab to open it, then noisily slurped up the drink that fizzed out onto the lid. "No way, Mandy," he said after he had swallowed the mouthful of soda. "You're getting carried away."

"No, seriously," Mandy insisted. "Ash could have been delivering the card, but not to Lydia."

"Who, then?" James took another gulp of soda.

"Jane," Mandy announced. "I think Andrew likes her. A lot. You saw how he blushed when we were talking about her earlier! Ash wasn't supposed to be at High Cross at all. He was supposed to take the card to Upper Welford Farm!"

Nine

"What a mix-up!" Mandy put her elbows on the table and cradled her chin in her hands. "The card ends up with the wrong person, who now thinks she's got a secret admirer, while the person who should have gotten it has no idea it was sent to her, and the person who sent it thinks the girl who should have gotten it isn't interested in him."

James blinked.

Mandy started again. "Lydia thinks someone likes her because she got an anonymous valentine. Andrew likes Jane and sent her a card. Jane never got it, but Andrew thinks she did, and now he's upset because Jane hasn't reacted to the card."

"If that's what really happened," James said doubtfully. "And anyway, why would Andrew send Jane a card with a goat on it? Goats aren't exactly romantic, and Lydia's the one who likes goats."

"Aha! So now you've changed your mind. You think Valentine's Day *should* be romantic." Mandy laughed triumphantly.

"I didn't say that at all," James protested. "Look, you might be right. About Jane being the one the card was meant for, I mean."

"And if I am, we're going to have to try to get the card to her. After all, it's our fault that she never got it in the first place."

"Our fault? Don't you mean *your* fault?" said James. "You're the one who saw Ash and called him over."

Mandy had to admit he was right. Ash hadn't wanted to give up the card, but Mandy had encouraged him until he did. "I really messed things up, didn't I?" she said sheepishly.

James put his head back and tipped the soda can upside down to drain the last few drops. Then he looked at Mandy again. "It's not too late to straighten things out. We could go to Lydia's tomorrow and offer to help out as usual. When we get a chance, we can sneak the card away and take it to Jane."

"Good idea."

"And I still think Valentine's Day is a load of mushy garbage," James quickly added.

"Oh sure." Mandy chuckled, giving him a sideways glance. She decided not to ask if he'd figured out who had sent him his own mystery card, in case he refused to help her take care of Lydia's situation.

"I feel kind of sorry for Lydia," Mandy said to James on their way up the path to Lydia's farmhouse the next day. "I'll bet she was happy to think someone liked her in that way."

James stood up on his pedals as the path grew steeper and bumpier. "I don't know about that," he said, puffing slightly. "Lydia's always telling us that she's happy with just her goats for company."

"That's what she wants us to think," Mandy said. "But I bet she wouldn't mind having a boyfriend."

This made James roar with laughter. "Lydia have a boyfriend? Never!"

And much as she would have liked to believe it was possible, Mandy had to agree that the idea of Lydia dating someone was a bit far-fetched. She was much more comfortable around goats than humans.

The two friends dropped their bikes on the ground in front of the farmhouse and knocked on the door. There was no reply, so Mandy guessed Lydia and Amy were in the barn. "We'll have to find some excuse to come back to the house and get the card," she said to James as they walked across the yard.

The barn door was open so they went right in. "Lydia? Amy? Are you in here?" Mandy called, peering into the darkness.

"Down at the end," came Lydia's voice. "We've just finished the milking."

"That's a shame," Mandy said, walking down the aisle between the rows of pens. "James and I came to help with that."

"Well, never mind," said Lydia, appearing with a bucket of fresh, foaming milk. There was a big hole in her sweater and when she saw Mandy staring at it, she grinned. "Houdini helped himself to a mouthful of wool! He obviously thought my sweater was tastier than his feed."

"Is there anything else we can do to help?" asked James.

"Oh definitely," said Lydia. "For one thing, someone needs to encourage Amy to do her homework. I can't seem to." Amy's teacher had given her some assignments to do while she was staying with her aunt so that she wouldn't fall behind her classmates. "As you can see, she'd rather work with the goats," said Lydia. She glanced behind her, and Mandy saw Amy leading Jemima back into her pen.

"Hi, you two," said Amy with a cheerful wave.

Mandy did a double take. Amy was starting to look just like her aunt! She was wearing faded blue jeans and a ratty old sweater with patches on the elbows. It hung so loosely on her — almost down to her knees — that Mandy guessed it belonged to Lydia. And the confident way in which Amy was handling Jemima made Mandy realize that she was as much at home with the goats as Lydia was. The chances of getting her to do her homework instead of spending time in the barn were probably pretty slim.

James offered to take the bucket from Lydia. "Want me to take this into the kitchen?" He gave Mandy a sideways glance so that she knew he wasn't just being polite.

"Oh, yes. That would —" Lydia began, but a spluttering, popping noise from outside interrupted her. "What's that?" she asked, going to the door.

The others followed and when they looked out, they saw Ernie's ancient van coming up the narrow driveway. It rattled and shook so much that Mandy thought it would fall apart, and every few seconds a loud bang came from its engine.

"It's backfiring," James explained. "That van needs a tune-up. Badly!"

"Do you think Ernie knows?" asked Amy.

"He must," said Lydia, shaking her head. There was a piece of straw clinging to her hair. She pulled it out, then looked down at the hole in her sweater. "Oh, dear, oh, dear," she muttered. "I can't go around like this!"

Mandy was surprised. A few moments ago Lydia hadn't been at all bothered by Houdini's handiwork!

"I'll have to change," Lydia continued and, still holding the bucket of milk, she rushed across the yard to the farmhouse.

"That's funny," Mandy remarked as they watched Lydia shut the kitchen door behind her.

"Yeah." Amy frowned. "She doesn't usually bother to get changed when people come to visit." Then her hands flew up to her mouth. "Hey! I've got it," she announced excitedly. "Aunt Lydia thinks Ernie's her secret admirer! That's why she's worried about what she looks like. And that's why she was so strange when Ernie came to fix the fence yesterday."

James pushed his glasses farther up on his nose. "You think so?"

"Yes." Amy nodded. "That's got to be it. The card's from Ernie, and Aunt Lydia knows that and she's really pleased. It's so romantic," she said dreamily.

"Oh, please," said James, groaning.

"Actually, we don't think the card's for Lydia after all," Mandy said. She explained their new theory, that Andrew had sent Ash to take it to Jane. "But you're probably on the right track about Lydia thinking Ernie sent her a valentine," she added.

Amy bit her lip. "That means Aunt Lydia's making a huge mistake." She looked anxiously toward the cottage, expecting Lydia to emerge at any moment. "She doesn't have a secret admirer after all."

Mandy glanced at James in dismay. The situation was getting out of hand! What on earth could they do to straighten things out without Lydia being horribly disappointed, or before she said something embarrassing to Ernie?

James made a face and shrugged as if to say, I don't know!

But there was no time to come up with a new plan. Ernie had almost reached the barn. His hands were behind his back, and he was smiling broadly, which struck Mandy as odd. Ernie was almost always frowning.

"Look at him!" Amy whispered. "He looks cheerful for a change. You know, I think he *does* like Aunt Lydia. Maybe this will all work out."

"Is Lydia around?" asked Ernie. "I've come to say I'm sorry about yesterday and — er — give her a present."

Amy looked delighted. "I bet he's got flowers, or chocolates," she whispered to Mandy. Then, to Ernie, she said out loud, "Aunt Lydia saw you coming, so she's gone to change."

Mandy wondered if Lydia would want Ernie to know that his arrival had prompted her to make herself presentable. Amy was obviously doing everything she could to fuel the romance!

"Oh, look, here she comes now," Amy went on eagerly.

Ernie coughed self-consciously as Lydia came across the yard.

Mandy blinked. In just a few minutes, Lydia had been completely transformed. Gone were the chewed-up sweater and the brown corduroy trousers. In their place were a soft pink sweater and a good-looking tweed skirt. And instead of boots, she was wearing neat brown shoes.

"Oh, hello, Ernie," said Lydia. She sounded as if she were surprised to see him, but her cheeks were bright red.

Mandy exchanged a guilty look with James. If she hadn't interfered with Andrew's card, things would make a lot more sense right now.

"Did you forget something yesterday?" Lydia asked Ernie.

Mandy wondered uncomfortably if she was referring to the card.

"Just my manners," replied Ernie. "So I've brought this for you." He took his hands out from behind his back with a flourish. "I thought you'd like it."

Out of the corner of her eye, Mandy saw Amy's shoulders sag and heard her utter a disappointed, "Oh, no!" The present was nothing like the romantic flowers and chocolates Amy had predicted. It was just a roll of paper.

"So much for all that sappy stuff," James muttered, giving Amy a meaningful look.

Lydia seemed disappointed, too, but she took the paper from Ernie and unrolled it. "What's this?" she asked, frowning, when she saw a lot of pencil drawings covering the page.

Ernie folded his arms across his chest and, looking rather pleased with himself, announced, "Plans for more goat pens in the barn. I drew them up myself."

Lydia studied the plans more closely. Mandy expected her to be annoyed, as she'd been when Ernie had told her she ought to increase her herd, but instead she smiled and said, "You old schemer, Ernie. You're determined for me to take Cartwright's goats, aren't you?"

"It's the only way, Lydia," he said. "If you want to survive in this business."

"Let's have a cup of tea and talk about it," Lydia said reasonably, which made Mandy exchange a hopeful glance with Amy.

They went into the house. When the tea was ready, instead of having it in the kitchen as usual, they went into the living room. Lydia sat on the sofa next to Ernie and spread the drawing out on the coffee table.

Ernie pointed to it with his stubby fingers. "You see, I thought if you put a row of pens down the center, there would still be room for a walkway on either side," he explained.

"That would mean room for, what, about a dozen more goats?" asked Lydia.

"At least. A couple more if you made the pens just that much smaller," said Ernie. "So you could easily take on Cartwright's herd."

Lydia was silent for a moment. Then she shook her head. "I'm not sure. It would mean an awful lot of extra work."

"It doesn't have to," said Ernie.

Lydia looked at him aghast. "Another dozen goats! Not extra work? Are you out of your mind, Ernie?"

"No, I think you could cope easily," replied Ernie.

"Yes, you could," said Amy, contradicting what she'd said yesterday when she'd backed up Lydia.

"Only if I was Superwoman," shot back Lydia.

"I'm not asking you to be Superwoman," Ernie argued. "Just sensible."

"Sensible?" Lydia was furious! She glared at Ernie. "Are you saying I'm not *sensible*, Ernie Bell?"

Mandy and Amy's eyes met again, this time in alarm. Was this the end of the romance already?

Lydia leaned forward and rolled up the drawing. "I'm sorry, Ernie. You shouldn't have bothered with this."

"Well, I did. And I still think you could manage if

you'd only ask for help. I could easily come up a few times a week."

"I don't think that would work, either," responded Lydia. "You have enough to do already." She stood up and went over to the mantelpiece. "I won't be taking on any more goats, and that's final." She slipped the plans behind the pewter mug, hiding the card from view, and then stood with her back to it, glowering at Ernie.

Oh, no, Mandy said to herself. *Now we'll never get that card. And everything else has gone wrong now, too.*

Because of the card, Lydia had expected Ernie to be romantic. But that was the last thing on his mind because he hadn't sent the card in the first place. And now the two were quarreling. But that wasn't all. If it hadn't been for the silly card, Ash and Major might never have fought in the yard at the dairy. And even though Major's condition had nothing to do with the fight, Ash's bad infection certainly did.

I wish Valentine's Day had never happened, Mandy thought unhappily.

Riding up the road to Animal Ark half an hour later, Mandy kept thinking of the way things had turned out. There wasn't going to be an easy solution to the mix-up, and with each passing day it was getting worse.

She sped up the driveway and stopped in front of the clinic just as Simon came out. He was on his way home, but he looked very worried.

"What's up?" Mandy asked, feeling her heart sink.

"It's Major," answered Simon. "He's —"

Mandy's heart skipped a beat. "He's what?"

Simon put his hand on her shoulder. "He's very sick," he said quietly. "Your mom and dad can't do anything else for him."

"You mean —" Mandy couldn't finish the sentence.

Simon nodded. "He'll have to be put to sleep, I'm afraid."

"But what about surgery?" Mandy found herself clutching at straws, just like Sam Western had done.

"Not an option in his case. For one thing, he's too old, and for another, your dad took some more X-rays this afternoon and they show that the heads of both of Major's femurs are way out of line with the sockets," Simon explained. "In fact, there's not much left of the sockets at all, poor dog."

Mandy was devastated. "Does Mr. Western know?"

"We've told him things are very bad. He should be here soon," said Simon.

Fifteen minutes later, Sam Western burst through the door. He looked distraught as he stood in front of the doctors while they explained the situation.

"I want a second opinion," he demanded when Dr. Adam said that the kindest thing for Major would be to put him out of his pain.

"Of course, you're entitled to one," said Dr. Adam. "But I think you'll get exactly the same diagnosis wherever you go. The most skilled surgeon in the world couldn't help Major now."

Mr. Western stared at the floor, and Mandy fought an urge to go and put her arms around him. She knew he was losing his best friend.

Dr. Emily pulled up a chair next to him. "I'm sorry, Mr. Western," she said kindly. "We know how much Major means to you."

Mandy nodded in silent agreement.

"Do you mind if I spend some time alone with him?" Mr. Western murmured.

"Take all the time you need," said Dr. Adam.

Looking very pale, Sam Western went into the residential unit. Mandy and her parents sat in the waiting room. No one spoke. After all, what was there to say?

After a while, Mr. Western came back in. His eyes were red and he swallowed hard before saying, "I'm ready." After Dr. Adam had gotten the necessary drug and a syringe, they all went back in to Major.

"You can hold him if you like," said Dr. Emily, and

Sam Western sat on the floor to lift his beloved companion into his lap.

Mandy crouched down and smoothed the old dog's fur. "You've had a good long life," she whispered, tears rolling freely down her cheeks. She wanted to say more, but she was sobbing too much and couldn't get the words out so she just looked into the German shepherd's eyes while she stroked his neck over and over.

Dr. Adam filled the syringe and then looked at Mr. Western. "Ready?"

Sam Western could only nod, then he looked away as the needle pierced the old dog's skin.

Moments later, it was all over and Major lay in his owner's arms, a look of peace on his handsome face as he fell asleep forever.

Ten

Every time an animal Mandy had cared for was put down, she felt a deep sense of loss. When she went into the residential unit the next morning and saw Major's empty cage, she couldn't stop the tears that poured from her eyes. "But at least he's not suffering anymore," she sobbed quietly before preparing herself to go and check on Ash.

Major's death had reminded her just how fragile life could be, and she was feeling much more gloomy about the collie's future. He'd been on medication for days now and was still no better. Last night, Dr. Emily had tried a different antibiotic, a lot stronger than the first. But would that make any difference at this stage?

Mandy came to Ash's cage and bent down. "How are —?" she began, then caught her breath. Ash was sitting up, looking at her with bright eyes and an alert expression on his beautiful face. He swished his tail from side to side and whined excitedly when Mandy reached through the wire to pat him.

Her spirits soared. "You're feeling better!"

Ash licked her hand and squirmed so that Mandy realized he needed to go outside. "Let's go for a walk," she said, opening the gate.

She took him out to the exercise track and he trotted around, sniffing the ground. He must have smelled something hidden in the grass because he began to dig eagerly, ignoring Mandy when she called out to him.

"Maybe you're hungry," she said, guessing that he might have detected a mole under the ground. She took him by the collar and led him back indoors to give him a bowl of food.

Ash didn't hesitate. He wolfed down his meal. Then, licking his lips, he looked at Mandy with his ears pricked as if asking for more.

"That's enough for now," Mandy smiled. Unable to stop herself from looking at the cage where Major had spent his last few days, she added, "You're a very lucky dog, you know that?" A new lump formed in her throat. She coughed and swallowed hard, and as she felt fresh tears pricking her eyes, she took Ash's dish and went to wash it, then busied herself by sweeping out his cage and changing his bedding.

Trying not to think about Major, she fed the other patients — a miniature poodle whose foot had been jammed in a door and a parakeet who'd been pulling out his feathers — before going to tell her mom and dad about Ash's recovery.

They were delighted to hear the good news.

"I had my fingers crossed that we'd see an improvement this morning," said Dr. Emily. "But I wasn't counting on it. That infection went on much too long for my liking."

"You obviously hit the nail on the head by changing the medication last night," said Dr. Adam, giving his wife a hug. "The bacteria causing the infection must have been resistant to the first antibiotic."

Mandy looked at her parents with admiration. "I hope I'll be as smart a vet someday as you two are," she said.

Dr. Adam chuckled. "You practically are already."

After seeing for herself that Ash was much better, Dr. Emily phoned Andrew and told him he could come over in the afternoon to take him home. Then, with patients starting to arrive, she and Dr. Adam went into their examining rooms to begin the morning's appointments.

Mandy was helping Jean to tidy the waiting area when ten-year-old Rachel Farmer arrived with her guinea pig, Hero. Even though Rachel didn't go to the same school as Mandy and James — she went to Welford Primary, in town — they knew her well.

"Hero has a sore claw," said Rachel, pointing it out to Mandy. "Mom thinks he might have caught it in the wire of his cage."

"He might have," Mandy agreed. She put her fingers through the mesh of the carrying case and scratched the little creature's head. "I don't think it's serious, though. It's not too swollen, and he's putting some weight on it."

Rachel was looking around the waiting room. "Is James here?" she asked.

"Not yet. He's coming over later to visit a collie named Ash," Mandy said. She'd phoned James to tell him that Ash was getting better at last and would be going home. James was as pleased with the news as Mandy and said he'd come over as soon as he'd finished cleaning his bedroom. Apparently, it was a mess and his mom had insisted he take care of it before going out.

"Oh," said Rachel, sounding rather disappointed. "Do you think" — she paused and bit her lip — "do you think," she went on in a rush, "that he got any valentine cards?"

Mandy was surprised. "Just one that I know of," she said. She was about to ask why Rachel wanted to know when the truth dawned on her. This must be James's secret admirer! But before she could ask Rachel if she'd sent the card, Jean interrupted them.

"Dr. Emily will see Hero now, if you'd like to take her in," she said, pointing to the door.

"See you later, Mandy," said Rachel.

Mandy could hardly wait for James to arrive now.

They were in the kitchen having some hot chocolate before going to see Ash when she told him that she had some important news.

"What is it?" asked James. He put down his mug expectantly.

"I know who sent you the valentine," Mandy announced.

"Oh, really?" James tried to sound as if he wasn't all that interested, but his ears had turned bright red. "Who?"

"Guess," said Mandy, enjoying herself too much to give away the answer so soon. "She lives in Welford, loves animals, and is a year younger than you."

"That could be lots of people," muttered James. He

gave Mandy an impatient look. "Come on, Mandy. Just say who it is."

"Rachel Farmer."

James blushed even more. "She was just playing a trick on me," he said. He gulped down another mouthful of hot chocolate, then pursed his lips and puffed as it scalded his tongue.

"Oh, no, she wasn't," Mandy said. "She was serious. You should have seen her face when she heard you weren't here."

"Come off it, Mandy. She doesn't like me," protested James.

"So, why the card?" Mandy persisted.

But James had had enough. "Cut it out, Mandy," he said hotly. "I don't like Rachel. Not in that way. She's just a friend. Like you are."

Mandy laughed. "Yeah, I bet."

"I *don't* have a crush on her!" James struck the table with the palm of his hand to stress his point. "*She* sent the card. Not me." He changed the subject. "Let's go and see Ash now," he said, and went to the door.

When the collie saw them coming, he stood up and pawed at the gate, whining. Now that he was well again, he was impatient to get out. "Later," Mandy promised. "But first, Andrew's got another important date."

"What's that?" asked James, crouching down to pet Ash. He stared at the collie in amazement as if he could hardly believe how much better he was.

"Well, we still have to fix the mix-up over the goat card," Mandy reminded him. "And I think I've figured out a good plan. But I have to make sure Jane's coming over today."

They found Simon in the pen in the backyard with a Staffordshire bull terrier puppy named Morsel. She had come in with a skin rash and was being tested for allergies.

"Do you know if Jane will be here later?" Mandy asked. She picked up a ball and threw it to the end of the run. The Staffie shot after it like a miniature torpedo.

"Yeah. She said she'd stop by after her shift at the dairy this afternoon."

"Perfect," Mandy said, winning the ball from Morsel's mouth and throwing it again.

"What's up?" Simon asked suspiciously. He crouched down and clapped his hands to encourage the little dog to come to him.

"Oh, nothing," Mandy said innocently.

"Here's Andrew," Mandy said when she saw his car coming up the driveway a few hours later. "He's just in time." She didn't only mean in time to get Ash before

Animal Ark closed for the night. "Come on, James. Let's go meet him."

They hurried outside.

"Hi, there," said Andrew, climbing out of his car. "Is everything OK?" A fleeting look of anxiety crossed his face as if he thought Mandy and James were greeting him with bad news.

"Just fine," Mandy smiled. "Ash looks great."

"And he can't wait to go home," added James.

"But first we have to tell you something," Mandy continued.

Andrew frowned and she quickly went on, "It's not about Ash. Well, it is," she said, "in a way." Even though she'd been turning the plan over and over in her mind all day, she suddenly felt embarrassed. She cleared her throat, shot James a pleading look in the hope he'd help out, then when he shook his head, she said, "You see, I made a big mistake the other day."

"You did?" Andrew looked surprised. "What kind of mistake?"

James took pity on Mandy and came straight to the point. "A valentine card mistake."

Andrew frowned. "Are you trying to say that you sent me a card by mistake?"

"No, that's not it." Mandy felt herself blushing. "No. It was the card you sent with Ash."

"You mean, the one with the goat on it?" Andrew asked slowly.

Now Mandy knew for sure that Andrew had sent his dog out to deliver the card. How else would he know it had a goat on it? She just hoped she was right about it being for Jane. If she wasn't, things could get even more embarrassing! "That's the one," she said. "Only it never got there."

"Got where?" Andrew looked closely at Mandy.

"To Upper Welford Hall?" Mandy's voice rose at the end of the sentence to show that she wasn't a hundred percent sure.

"She means to Jane," cut in James.

Andrew's expression was filled with a host of emotions. At first he looked as embarrassed as Mandy, but when she told him how she'd intercepted Ash on his mission and taken the card from him and given it to Lydia, he said, "Well, that explains everything," and the embarrassment faded and he looked relieved, and even amused. He began to laugh, then stopped. "Poor Lydia. It's going to be a bit rough on her when she finds out she doesn't have a secret admirer."

"It's worse than that," Mandy admitted. "She thinks Ernie sent the card."

"Not that that matters," James added. "The two of

them have been bickering nonstop for days now. I don't think Valentine's Day did anything for them."

"Since when did you think Valentine's Day mattered anyway?" Mandy couldn't resist asking him.

James made a face at her, and Mandy continued, "I still think Lydia and Ernie might like each other. I mean, she didn't throw the plans away, did she?"

Andrew looked baffled. "What plans?"

"For new goat pens," said James. Then he answered Mandy. "No. She hid them behind the mug with the card," he recalled.

"Anyway, we'll just have to hope that they work things out themselves," Mandy said and, giving James an almost invisible nudge, she added to Andrew, "You don't want to be bothered with all this now. The main thing is that Ash is better and you've come to take him home."

"Yes, definitely," said Andrew, sounding very pleased.

"Come on," she said, pushing open the door to the reception area. She glanced over her shoulder at Andrew. "By the way, why did you send a card with a *goat* on it?"

"Because of a joke I had with Jane a few weeks ago." Andrew wiped his feet on the mat before going inside. "I told her that I thought I didn't have a ghost of a chance with her, and she misheard me and thought I said *goat* of a chance, which obviously didn't make any sense at all. So when I saw the card in a store, I knew it was perfect because she was sure to know it was from me. And that's why I was a bit annoyed when she didn't say anything on Valentine's Day."

"You didn't know she never got it," said James.

"No, but I was pretty certain she had. You see, she goes for a walk on the field most afternoons, so I sent Ash out in the direction she always takes."

"Well, never mind that now." Mandy was almost bursting with excitement. She pushed open the door to the residential unit and stood aside to let Andrew go in. "There's someone waiting to see you." And just before she closed the door behind Andrew she caught a glimpse of Jane looking up from where she was kneeling beside Ash's cage.

"Nice one." James chuckled as they went back into the reception area. "Making Jane think we couldn't be around to get Ash ready to go home." The two friends had pretended they'd be out that afternoon and had asked Jane to make sure Ash was ready for Andrew to take him home. It was the only way Mandy could think of to get Jane and Andrew alone.

"I think we'd better get away from here before those two come out," said Mandy. "I'm tired of seeing people blushing!"

But just as they were going out, they heard Simon calling them. "Do you know if Jane's still here?" he asked, coming into the reception area.

"Yes, she is. Why?" Mandy asked hesitantly. They didn't need Simon to go bursting in and interrupt Jane and Andrew now.

"I thought I'd ask her to the movies," he said.

Mandy groaned and James rolled his eyes. All these romantic intrigues were becoming a bit much!

"Er, I think it's a bit late for that," Mandy said, and when Simon looked disappointed she plowed on. "You see, Andrew's probably asking her the same sort of thing right now." Then she and James fled, with Mandy making up her mind to leave things like this to luck — or Cupid — in the future!

The next time Mandy saw Ash was the following Saturday at the market in the town square. The collie looked magnificent as he trotted along next to Andrew. He wasn't even limping, and the ear that had been so injured was standing up as straight and strong as the good one. But that wasn't all that gave Mandy a warm glow, for walking arm in arm with Andrew was Jane!

"It worked out perfectly," Mandy said to James and Amy.

The three friends were helping Lydia with her booth,

which had goat's milk for sale and also pretty baskets with their heart-shaped cheeses and hand lotion. Blackie had come along, too, and he barked when he saw his new friend, but James held on to his collar tightly.

"I wonder when they'll be getting married?" Amy said dreamily as she watched Andrew and Jane threading their way through the crowd at the market.

James rolled his eyes. "Honestly! A guy sends someone a card and next thing you know, everyone thinks they're getting married."

"You never know." Mandy chuckled, risking a quick look at Lydia who was talking to a customer about the benefits of goat's milk. "I mean, it could happen to you, James," she teased as she noticed someone else approaching the stall. "Look who's coming."

"Rachel! Oh, no." James gasped. He looked around in panic. "Quick, I need to hide!" He dove under the table among the cardboard boxes and crates of milk bottles, dragging a very astonished Blackie with him. "Keep still, boy," came his muffled voice.

He'd just vanished when Rachel reached the booth. "Hi, Mandy. Hi, Amy. Has anyone seen James?"

"Er" — Mandy began, and she felt James's elbow in her shin — "I think he's looking for some —"

"Some boxes or something," Amy finished with a grin.

"Oh. Well, I guess I'll see him around sometime," said Rachel, and then she saw the heart-shaped cheeses. "These are so nice!" she exclaimed, taking a change purse out of her pocket. "I'll definitely buy one, to give to someone special."

A low groan escaped from under the table, and even though Mandy was amused, she showed her loyalty to her best friend by coughing loudly to cover up his voice.

Next to arrive at the booth were Andrew, Jane, and Ash. Both Jane and Andrew looked happier than ever, but it was Ash who stole the show, gazing up at the familiar friends with his long, pointed face, striped with perfectly symmetrical flashes of white.

"Hello, gorgeous!" Mandy said, kneeling in front of him.

As if to show her just how well he was feeling, Ash jumped up and put his front paws on her shoulders, nearly tipping her over.

"No, you don't," said Andrew, gently pulling the dog off. "That shows very bad manners."

But Mandy didn't mind in the least. It took a lot for her to be angry with an animal, especially one who'd been so badly injured.

From under the table, a small voice said, "Is it OK to come out now?"

"Yup. The coast is clear," Mandy told James. He stood up cautiously and looked around to make sure Rachel had gone.

Jane frowned. "What were you doing under there?"

"Er, checking the boxes," said James, which made Mandy and Amy burst out laughing.

The two dogs were delighted to meet again. They sniffed each other's faces, and even though their owners were holding them on their leashes, they started to jump around each other playfully.

"Steady," Mandy said. "We don't want any of those stitches coming out yet."

"He's certainly bounced back well, hasn't he?" said Lydia, admiring the sleek collie. Then, out of the blue, she blushed a deep red that clashed with the yellow sweater she was wearing. "Oh, dear," she said, looking rather flustered.

Mandy couldn't imagine what was causing Lydia such discomfort until she saw Ernie walking purposefully across the green. He was wearing a neat tweed jacket and a brand-new cap, which he took off when he was a few feet away from the stall.

"Afternoon, everyone," he said gruffly. Then, looking

straight at Lydia, he said, "I'm not one for beating around the bush and wasting time. Are you going to take on those extra goats or not?"

Lydia didn't seem to know what to say. "I, um, you know, I —" she began.

But Ernie meant what he said about not beating around the bush. "The thing is," he paused, sounding gruffer than ever, "will you marry me?"

Mandy could have been knocked down with a feather! James looked just as astonished, while Amy said triumphantly, "I knew it!"

"Marry you!" Lydia's eyes were like saucers. "What makes you think I would marry you? You're as stubborn and as awkward as Houdini."

There was an unexpected twinkle in Ernie's eye, and his voice grew softer. "That's exactly why I think we'd get along," he said, which made Lydia smile and her face light up.

"I'll say yes on one condition. And that's if you promise to have that old van of yours repaired. I won't be seen dead in a sputtery old thing like that."

"It's as good as done," said Ernie, and he dared to lean forward and peck Lydia on her cheek.

"And one other thing," said Lydia, when she'd recovered from the surprise of the kiss. "If you're such a straight talker, why didn't you sign that crazy card?"

Ernie looked at her blankly. "Eh?"

Oops, thought Mandy, then quickly said out loud, "Yes, well, that wasn't quite what it seemed. We'll explain everything some other time." She hoped that in all the excitement, the matter of the misplaced card would soon be forgotten.

A starry-eyed Amy was glancing from Andrew and Jane to Lydia and Ernie, then back again. "It's all so romantic," she breathed.

"And don't forget Rachel and James," Mandy said, chuckling mischievously.

"Cut it out," said James, punching her on the arm. As he did, he let go of Blackie's leash. This was exactly what the Labrador had been waiting for. With an excited bark, he leaped at Ash, then whirled around and bounded away, inviting the collie to chase him.

Ash responded in a flash. He jerked his leash free as well, and streaked after Blackie, the two dogs knocking into booths and making people jump out of their way.

"Come back here, you two!" shouted James, and then the blood drained from his face, like a reverse blush, when he saw Blackie and Ash skid to a halt in front of Rachel Farmer.

"Don't worry. I've got him!" Rachel called, beaming with delight as she took hold of Blackie's collar and began leading him back to James.

"Oh, no." James groaned. There was no way he could dive under the table now.

"You'll just have to be straight, like Ernie." Mandy grinned. "Tell her you're not interested." She watched Rachel hurrying happily across the grass, with Blackie trotting along next to her in an unbelievably obedient way.

To Mandy's delight, Ash was walking behind, exactly as if he was herding them back to James. The collie was panting slightly, looking to all the world as if he was grinning. And there was a purposefulness about him that made Mandy realize that Ash was more than just a maildog—a collie with a card. He was a matchmaking dog who wasn't going to be happy until everyone in Welford had met their perfect match!

Read all the Animal Ark books!

Where animals come first

by Ben M. Baglio

$3.99 US Each!

- ❏ BDB 0-439-09700-2 **Bunnies in the Bathroom**
- ❏ BDB 0-439-34407-7 **Cat in a Crypt**
- ❏ BDB 0-439-34393-3 **Cats at the Campground**
- ❏ BDB 0-439-34413-1 **Colt in the Cave**
- ❏ BDB 0-439-34386-0 **Dog at the Door**
- ❏ BDB 0-439-34408-5 **Dog in the Dungeon**
- ❏ BDB 0-439-23021-7 **Dolphin in the Deep**
- ❏ BDB 0-439-34415-8 **Foal in the Fog**
- ❏ BDB 0-439-34385-2 **Foals in the Field**
- ❏ BDB 0-439-23018-7 **Guinea Pig in the Garage**
- ❏ BDB 0-439-09701-0 **Hamster in a Handbasket**
- ❏ BDB 0-439-34387-9 **Horse in the House**
- ❏ BDB 0-439-44891-3 **Hound at the Hospital**
- ❏ BDB 0-439-44897-2 **Hound on the Heath**
- ❏ BDB 0-439-09698-7 **Kitten in the Cold**
- ❏ BDB 0-590-18749-X **Kittens in the Kitchen**
- ❏ BDB 0-439-34392-5 **Mare in the Meadow**
- ❏ BDB 0-590-66231-7 **Ponies at the Point**
- ❏ BDB 0-439-34388-7 **Pony in a Package**
- ❏ BDB 0-590-18750-3 **Pony on the Porch**
- ❏ BDB 0-439-34391-7 **Pup at the Palace**
- ❏ BDB 0-590-18751-1 **Puppies in the Pantry**
- ❏ BDB 0-439-34389-5 **Puppy in a Puddle**
- ❏ BDB 0-590-18757-0 **Sheepdog in the Snow**
- ❏ BDB 0-439-34126-4 **Stallion in the Storm**
- ❏ BDB 0-439-34390-9 **Tabby in the Tub**
- ❏ BDB 0-439-44892-1 **Terrier in the Tinsel**

Available wherever you buy books, or use this order form.

Scholastic Inc., P.O. Box 7502, Jefferson City, MO 65102

Please send me the books I have checked above. I am enclosing $_____ (please add $2.00 to cover shipping and handling). Send check or money order—no cash or C.O.D.s please.

Name _____ Age _____

Address _____

City _____ State/Zip _____

Please allow four to six weeks for delivery. Offer good in the U.S. only. Sorry, mail orders are not available to residents of Canada. Prices subject to change.

More Series You'll Fall in Love With

Heartland™

Nestled in the foothills of Virginia, there's a place where horses come when they are hurt. Amy, Ty, and everyone at Heartland work together to heal the horses—and form lasting bonds that will touch your heart.

The AMAZING DAYS of ABBY HAYES®

In a family of superstars, it's hard to stand out. But Abby is about to surprise her friends, her family, and most of all, herself!

Jody is about to begin a dream vacation on the wide open sea, traveling to new places and helping her parents with their dolphin research.

You can tag along with **Dolphin Diaries**

Available Wherever Books Are Sold.

■SCHOLASTIC

www.scholastic.com

GIR